WE DRANK WINE

AND OTHER STORIES

Author Photo: Trina Koster Photography
Cover Art: Write Design

Library and Archives Canada Cataloguing in Publication

Reidel, Marion, 1955-
[Short stories. Selections]
    We drank wine : and other stories / Marion Reidel.

Issued in print and electronic formats.
ISBN 978-1-927890-12-7 (softcover).--
ISBN 978-1-927890-13-4 (HTML)

    I. Title.

PS8635.E45A6 2017   C813'.6   C2017-904604-7
                                         C2017-904605-5

Printed in United States of America

Published by Sun Dragon Press Inc., Canada
www.sundragonpress.com
First Edition, 2017

WE DRANK WINE

AND OTHER STORIES

Marion Reidel

Dedication

This book is dedicated to my family;
Tom, Katie, John and my "Bent Elbow" sisters.
Their support made the difference.

Acknowledgements

This collection has been three years in the making. Creating these stories has been entertaining and offered new experiences. Writing provided the opportunity to join Guelph's vibrant writing community, the members of which offered the feedback and support necessary to refine my work.

Thank you to the teachers who guided me. Melinda Burns, Nikki Evertt-Hammond, Marilyn Kleiber and Brian Henry all played significant roles in mentoring me through this work. Through them, peers work-shopped the pieces with compassion and insight.

The in-progress editing services of Nancy Fischer, Anastasia McEwen and Annette Yaskowich served to make my work presentable. It's impossible to see one's own errors and their keen eyes kept shame at bay.

Thanks to Lisa Browning of *One Thousand Trees* and the Eden Mills Writers' Festival, for opportunities to publicize my work. Winning the Eden Mills Fringe Contest, and then their Literary Contest, were pivotal events in building confidence.

A special mention must also go out to *Guelph Spoken Word*. Their writing workshops, and the regular opportunity to test my work in front of a live audience, played an important role in refining this work. Bringing these stories to life through presentation has been a huge source of pleasure in my life. Guelph's diverse spoken word community has made me feel welcome and honoured me with inclusion in their Guelph Comedy Festival performance.

My gratitude goes out to Art Kilgour of *Write Design*. He understood my vision for the cover artwork and patiently handled my need for full control. His sense of colour and design resulted in a perfect visual representation.

This book became a reality through the services of *Sun Dragon Press.* Marilyn Kleiber understood my work and was not afraid to tell me when it required changes. Her editorial expertise, encouragement and belief in the value of this work brought this project to completion.

Contents

Once Bitten — 1

Hell on Heels — 7

Bedtime Story — 13

Septic Hot Tub — 23

I'm Just A Girl — 29

No Satisfaction — 33

We Drank Wine — 41

Therapy — 53

Amber Alert — 61

Alpha Male — 67

Call of Support — 75

Mother-of-the-Bride — 81

Wedding Toast — 89

The Fireman — 97

Breaking Through — 109

A Short Drive — 115

Adopt-a-Pet — 127

High Tea for Two — 135

Double Chocolate Toffee Delight — 149

Let's Pretend — 155

I Saved Someone's Life — 163

Viking Cruise — 171

Caribbean Getaway — 183

Marion Reidel

Once Bitten

Being a parent is the hardest job I ever tackled. Well, being a wife is difficult too, and being an adult daughter is no piece of cake. I decided I could do the job better than my parents, so I charged ahead unaware of how my every action would shape the life of another human being. I wasn't alone in this task. Throughout the ordeal, I had the support of three good friends. We've been through all kinds of challenges together, but parenting… that's been the biggest.

Our kids were around the same age. Thank goodness, the two eldest were in school by the time we started the Monday Morning Mother's Group. Celeste came up with the idea. She had a daughter, Tiffany, and a son, Geoffrey. Everything about her life seemed perfect. Her husband owned a business and they lived in a huge house. Mine would fit in their two-car garage. Tiffany, a clone of her mother, was a precocious blue-eyed, blonde angel who always wore dresses with patent leather Mary-Janes and lace-trimmed ankle socks. She loved the Harry Potteresque uniform at the private school she attended and at seven years old had reduced one of her teachers to tears by questioning her instructional methodology. She took ballet lessons, and played piano.

Celeste's son Geoffrey was four, so he participated in the Monday Morning Mother's Group. Celeste always called him by his full name; she would accept nothing less. She dressed him in button-down shirts with clip-on bow ties when the other kids wore Ninja Turtle T-shirts. Geoffrey hated having sticky fingers and needed his hair perfectly in place. I couldn't be sure if Geoffrey's fussiness was his doing, or his mother's.

Geoffrey did not enjoy sharing toys. He and his sister each had their own gender-specific items, to minimize conflict. But at the Monday Morning Mother's Group my Taylor couldn't wait to get her hands on Geoffrey's Tonka trucks and construction sets, and he didn't like it one little bit. Celeste assured me that she formed the Monday Morning Mother's Group so our children could have the opportunity to interact with their peers. And besides, she said her housekeeper would handle any conflicts.

Geoffrey's possessiveness frustrated Taylor and so… the biting began. She would pick up a toy he wasn't using, and Geoffrey would stomp over to retrieve it. When Geoffrey grabbed it, Taylor would refuse to let go, and one day, when he kept tugging, she bit his forearm. At least that's what Celeste's housekeeper reported. We were in the living room drinking Mimosas, but the teeth marks on Geoffrey's arm verified her story.

All the children in the group learned to fear my daughter's bite. Sandy also had two kids. Her son Devon, a moody four year old, had dark eyes and hair like his father. Everyone considered Sandy's husband, Robert, outrageously handsome. His family ran a contracting firm, making Robert the only one of our husbands involved in manual labour. It showed in his physique. He'd always been fit and tanned, with a smile that could melt a glacier. Devon looked like Robert, but lacked the charm. Sandy said Devon suffered from second child syndrome. Her daughter Amber, who attended kindergarten, overpowered Devon verbally and physically, so he learned to retreat. I've seen Devon sit in a corner and play with a single block because the other kids wouldn't share. Sandy used to say his behavior indicated a high degree of creativity. She thought he'd grow up to be a writer, musician, or maybe even an actor. I thought she was projecting her own lost dreams on the poor kid. I'd describe Devon as shy and a bit of a social victim, even for Taylor who was a year younger.

Besides Geoffrey, Devon and Taylor, one more kid attended the group. Angela, the oldest at seven, was home schooled by Janice, Celeste's neighbour. It surprised me when Celeste included Janice because she would not normally socialize with Janice's type. When I asked Celeste about it, she acted like she didn't understand, but it seemed suspicious. Janice talked a lot, a trait Celeste rarely tolerated. She liked people to be clear and concise, but Janice sort of rambled and dominated the conversation. Janice could also be described as… well… fat is the only way to say it. She claimed her extra weight resulted from Angela's birth, but really, that was seven years ago. I think Janice had let herself go. Her husband, Trevor, didn't seem to mind. We met him at a poolside BBQ and he gushed over Janice all evening. They had a backyard pool we all loved.

Taylor bit Angela. I witnessed the incident. We were giving the kids a snack, so they were all sitting nicely at the peninsula in Celeste's open-concept kitchen. Each child had a cup of apple juice and a plate with two chocolate chip cookies, homemade by Celeste's housekeeper. Angela gobbled hers down and then grabbed the second one from Taylor's plate. Without hesitation, Taylor leaned over and bit Angela on the upper arm, took the cookie back and continued eating with a cookie in each hand. For a second I hoped no one had noticed, but Angela screeched and there on her arm, for everyone to see, sat a little red circle of teeth marks.

It's only natural for a parent to feel responsible for their child's behaviour, even when they are only three years old. It was one thing to have Taylor assault the children of my closest friends, but she also did it at Kindergym when a boy butted in line, at preschool when a girl took the spot she wanted in the story circle and at the playground when a bigger kid tried to get her off the swing. I had to do something about it.

Like I said, parenting is hard. I didn't know what to do about Taylor, but worse than that, everyone seemed to have firm opinions about the proper course of action. Janice suggested using treats to reinforce positive behaviour. If Taylor played nicely with others, waited her turn, shared her toys, then I gave her a Smartie. I carried a bag of them in my pocket and doled them out like puppy treats. *Good girl, have a Smartie.* I had to give up that technique when the other kids saw me and demanded treats for themselves.

Sandy said I should ignore it. She had read toddlers bite as a result of frustration and eventually, when Taylor developed a better vocabulary, she would use her words to express herself and the biting would stop. No big deal, she said. But during story time at the public library Dougie Stevens pestered Taylor, so she bit him on the arm and broke the skin. Dougie's mother, Stella, is a nurse and made a point of telling me human bites are full of bacteria. She took Dougie to get shots. I had to buy Stella a bottle of premium red wine to keep her from gossiping.

Then, Celeste stepped up with the ultimate solution. She placed a hand on my shoulder and said, "Beth, in order for Taylor to understand that biting is unacceptable, she needs to experience being bitten herself." I had no practical way to get one of the other kids to bite Taylor. Celeste said I would have to do the dirty deed myself, immediately after the next incident. As I look back, I can't believe I accepted the theory that I should bite my own kid to stop her from biting. It felt like hitting a kid to say stop hitting, or telling a teen not to smoke with a cigarette hanging from your lip. Somehow, at the time, it seemed like the only solution.

Once I had embraced Celeste's strategy, Taylor took a hiatus from her oral attacks. In hindsight, this reprieve lulled me into complacency and so I reacted badly to her surprise attack. We had a fabulous day at the pool. Sandy, Amber and Devon joined us and the kids played together perfectly. They splashed in the shallow end, and jumped in using their water wings, then we had a picnic in the shade. It seemed joyous… until we left.

Sandy had already packed her two into her van and she just pulled out of the lot when Taylor had a meltdown. She didn't want to leave the pool. She was hot, overtired and had consumed too much sugar. The ingredients combined to send her over the edge and she threw herself on the pavement beside our car. She caused such a scene I looked around to see if there were any witnesses. I feared someone would think I was abducting a child as I forcibly strapped Taylor into the backseat. That's when she bit me, hard, on my fore-arm. It hurt. I felt tired and frustrated and so… I bit her back. But I did it very carefully. I took her tiny arm in my hands and I looked her in the eye. I said to her, "It is not nice to bite people. It hurts. Like this." And then I bit her. Not hard enough to break her skin, but I could clearly see the indents of my teeth on her perfect flesh.

Taylor looked at me, her blue eyes magnified by tears. She seemed to stop breathing for a second, then went silent. She didn't yell. She didn't cry. She didn't express any form of displeasure. My own behavior shocked me. I buckled Taylor into the car and climbed behind the wheel. I put on her favourite tape and sang to her all the way home.

Taylor and I never spoke about it. In fact, I've never told anyone, until now. I have no idea whether she can remember, but Taylor gave up biting and I began carrying around a little bundle of parental guilt I've been adding to as the years go by.

Hell on Heels

A visit with my best friend never fails to deteriorate my carefully crafted self-confidence. She enlisted me as her side-kick during university and I have been a loyal member of her entourage ever since. She dragged me up the social ladder and molded me to approximate her sense of style, while I fed her ever-hungry ego. We were co-dependent; a relationship from which neither of us felt motivated to escape.

I refer to Celeste as my best friend because she consistently reminds me of my status as hers. She says things like, "Since you're my best friend, Sandy, I'm sure you'd like to look after my kids on Tuesday mornings, while I go to yoga class." Or on another occasion she said, "Sandy, I could never let my best friend leave the house looking like that. Let's do something about your hair." And I'll never forget the day when she told me, "Honey, as your best friend, I have to tell you it's time to lose that baby weight. I can count two dinner rolls in addition to your muffin tops." She means well.

As her number one, Celeste recruited me to stand at her side the day she decided to take on the *Always Helping Others League*. They were an uppity bunch of stay-at-home mothers, affluent enough to buy their freedom by employing housekeepers and nannies. They met Wednesday mornings, in the country club's boardroom, to plan charitable fundraisers while propagating neighbourly gossip. They were an exclusive group and Celeste intended to penetrate their enclave. Their resistance… was futile.

Celeste made several attempts to secure an official invitation. Our husbands had golf memberships at the club and Celeste hinted about her interest while attending League events. She also expressed her desire during Bridge afternoons at a League member's home. Celeste suspected the current Chairperson had blacklisted her because the Chair's husband spent too much time offering Celeste assistance at the driving range. She decided the situation required a more aggressive approach. We'd just show up at their meeting.

"You want to go, uninvited?" I asked without any attempt to hide my dismay. I refilled Celeste's glass of merlot and took my place on her living room couch.

"It's the perfect plan," she replied. Smirking, she raised her glass and held it up to the plate glass window, twirling the stem between her professionally manicured fingertips, and admiring the rich burgundy hue. "Those gals have impeccable manners. They're very conscious of how they are perceived, so they couldn't possibly make a scene. They'll be forced to welcome us graciously."

"Us?"

"Of course. You don't think I'd go without my best friend?" Celeste laughed and took a sip of her wine. Her lips, the same shade of red as her nails, left a kiss on the rim of her Mikasa stemware. "We'll take them by surprise and they'll be unable to refuse our participation."

We spent three days preparing for the infiltration. Celeste's husband was significantly more successful than mine, so our new dresses went on her credit card. She selected a full skirt to hide my hips and a body-hugging classic to show off hers.

At the Sweet Retreat Spa, we were waxed and polished

like fine furniture. Our hair was sculpted and lacquered, and my nails gained half a centimeter which buttressed my confidence. Celeste was in her element while being attended to. She blossomed like a hot house rose, tight, delicate and almost too perfect to believe.

Celeste's most devastating weapons were attached to her feet. On the morning of the meeting she suggested I drive. She said her footwear wasn't gas pedal friendly. Taking the passenger seat turned out to be a choreographed strategy to enhance her arrival at the club's main entrance. The concierge opened the car door and Celeste extended long, smooth legs accoutered with bright red, open-toed Louboutin heels. She was armed and dangerous.

There's something about the engineering of stiletto heels that did more than just add inches to Celeste's presence. They realigned her spine, tightened her butt and created a stern posture. Her form-fitting dress enforced a modest stride and the heels of her shoes clicked decisively as she crossed the terrazzo foyer to the boardroom.

Our approach went unheeded by the League members. It was timed perfectly. They were filling coffee mugs and pulling up chairs as we breezed into the room and merged with their movements. Celeste smiled and greeted the women adjacent to her by name. We poured ourselves a coffee, sat at the table and struck an attentive pose. Celeste crossed her legs and let one Louboutin bounce.

A brief flurry of whispers and glances swept through the room, then the chairperson tapped her gavel and silence settled. No one asked why we were there. I suspect each wondered if someone else invited us. The minutes of the previous meeting were read and approved, some housekeeping matters addressed and then Celeste prepared to take her shot.

Margaret Abernathy, a sagging sixty-something currently serving as League chairperson, opened the discussion about their next event. "It has been suggested we revisit the garden party format that worked so well last year. Although it's our most successful event financially, the challenge is that Party Central has increased their tent rental fee by 50%."

"It's outrageous," said Caroline Smith-Harding, who then cast her gaze around the room to invite murmurs of agreement. "How are we expected to raise a significant amount for the Youth Literacy Breakfast Program, if our costs escalate?"

An unfocused discussion sprung from this question, during which a variety of members moaned and whined. The secretary tried to capture every comment and the Chair seemed oblivious to the random and pointless nature of the interaction. I saw a practiced look of sympathy pasted on Celeste's face.

After letting the group ramble for a while, Celeste raised her manicured hand in a gesture reminiscent of a ballet move. The slight inward curl of her pinky and ring fingers ensured that those seated on either side of her caught the flash of red on her fingertips. The back of her hand was turned so the track lighting caused her diamond to sparkle, and her wrist flexed to encourage the collection of bangles to fall in a jangling cluster. "Excuse me," she said.

Margaret acknowledged her presence with, "Celeste, what a delightful surprise to see you and your friend Sandra. How can we help you this morning?"

"Well, Madam Chair, it is my hope I will be able to help

you," Celeste countered. "You see my husband's company is looking for a means of making a charitable donation. Perhaps they could cover the cost of the tent and furnishings for our event."

As the group erupted into supportive chatter, Celeste slowly rose from her seat and strode to the whiteboard behind Margaret, at the head of the table. She smiled as she towered over the Committee Chair, and took a marker in her hand. I leaned back in my seat and beamed with admiration as Celeste drew a rough seating plan, indicating tent size requirements and table numbers.

Margaret rolled her seat out of the way as Celeste smoothly took over management of the meeting. An hour later, as her clicking heels receded from the country club, I followed Celeste to the car, grateful to be her best friend.

Marion Reidel

Bedtime Story

"Why are we doing this?"

"I want to enhance your general aptitude for learning. This will advance your vocabulary, help you grasp concepts and understand cause and effect relationships. It will have a positive impact on all facets of your education."

"Dad, I'm nine years old. I can read to myself."

"Researchers suggest that listening to someone read builds capacity for paying attention and self-discipline. Interpersonal contact strengthens communication skills and solidifies the parent-child bond."

Taylor rolled her eyes and sighed. In her hands was a bright pink paperback with an artist's rendering on the cover showing an angry teenaged girl in the foreground and three girls whispering behind her. Taylor succumbed to her father's will, inserted a bookmark, then set her book on her night table. "Okay, but pull up a chair. There's not enough room on my bed for the both of us."

Randall removed stray clothes from the chair next to Taylor's closet. He pretended not to notice the floral underpants drift to the carpet as he placed the pile carefully on top of her dresser. He moved the chair so the bedside lamp would illuminate his book.

"I'm your only kid. I don't know how our bond could be any stronger," said Taylor. She stacked her pillows against the headboard and pulled her knees up under the covers. "What book do you have?"

"I borrowed this from the children's department at the library," said Randall. He held a large, dark, hardcover volume. Its edges were frayed and the embossed gold lettering was so worn it would hardly be seen. "It's an anthology of classic folk tales for children."

Taylor groaned. "I am not a child. Why don't you read from mine? It's the third book in the Summerhill Junior High series. It's really good."

"I'll leave that for you. The story I have selected is called 'Boots, Who Ate a Match with the Troll.' It's not very long. Let's begin." Randall opened the book and cleared his throat. He was proud of his oratorical skills. He'd competed in several public speaking contests during university and belonged to the local Toastmaster's club. Randall knew he could win over his daughter.

"Once upon a time there was a farmer, who had three sons; his means were small, and he was old and weak, and his sons would take to nothing."

"How come they're all sons? Why isn't there a daughter in the story? That's kinda sexist isn't it?"

"It's an old story. Written before people understood about gender equity."

"Change one of the sons to a daughter then. The third one, 'cuz I bet that's the good one."

"Okay… *Once upon a time there was a farmer, who had two sons and a daughter; his means were small, and he was old and weak, and his children would take to nothing. A fine large wood belonged to the farm, and one day the father told his sons...* and daughter… *to go and hew wood, and try to pay off some of his debts."*

"Hew wood?"

"Chop wood."

"Then why didn't you say that?"

"It is a classic tale written in old-fashioned language. Just listen… *Well, after a long talk, he got them to set off, and the eldest was to go first. But when he got well into the wood…*"

"He went inside the wood?" Taylor scrunched up her nose as if she had smelled something offensive.

"He went into the forest. Wood, woods, means forest."

"Then why don't you say forest? This story is not very clear."

"Give it a chance. *But when he got well into the…* forest, *and began to hew…* I mean chop… *at a mossy old fir…* that's a type of evergreen tree, not the hair on an animal… *when what should he see coming up to him but a great sturdy Troll.*" Randall paused to evaluate his daughter's reaction.

"You mean like my dolls? The ones with the colourful hair that sticks straight up?"

"Maybe. It doesn't say what he looks like."

"Was he naked? My trolls are naked."

"I suspect he wore some form of crude clothing. May I proceed? *If you hew…* chop… *this wood…* forest… *of mine, said the Troll, I'll kill you.*"

"I thought the farmer owned forest."

"Perhaps no one told the Troll that."

"Wouldn't the troll be an indigenous person? Maybe the farmer expropriated the land from the Troll?" Taylor pretended to scratch her cheek to hide her smirk.

"Where did you learn about expropriating land from indigenous people?"

"At school."

"It think it is faulty logic to apply a contemporary analysis to a folk tale," said Randall. He took a deep breath and flipped the page to reassure himself of the story's brevity. "Why don't I just read, without interruption, and we can debrief the story at the end? Okay?"

"Okay… but I think threatening to kill someone over cutting a tree is a bit of an overreaction. That Troll should take a chill pill." Taylor grinned.

Randall raised an eyebrow, but decided not to respond. *"When the lad heard that, he threw the ax down, and ran off home as fast as he could lay legs to the ground…"* Taylor opened her mouth to speak, but Randall intercepted her thought. "No, he did not actually take off his legs and lay them on the ground. It is a poetic way of saying that he ran fast. … *so he came in quite out of breath, and told them what happened, but his father called him a 'hare-heart' – no Troll would ever have scared him from chopping wood when he was young, he said."*

"Not a very supportive father." Taylor held eye contact with Randall for a moment before he continued.

"Next day the second son's turn came, and he feared just the same. He had scarcely chopped three strokes at the tree, before the Troll came up to him too, and said, If you cut this forest of mine, I'll kill you."

"I see a pattern here," said Taylor.

Randall smiled, thinking he had engaged his daughter in the tale. *"The lad dared not so much as look at him, but threw down the ax, took to his heels, and went scampering home just like his brother. When he got home, his father was angry again and said no Troll had ever scared him when he was young."*

"What the father should be mad about is the axes."

"Pardon?"

"The sons. They both dropped their ax in the forest and left it there. Now the family is running out of axes and the Troll is pretty heavily armed. That's something to worry about," said Taylor.

"Hmmm." Randall did not want to encourage a divergent discussion so he pressed on. *"The third day Boots wanted to set off."*

"That's the daughter," said Taylor.

"Yes," replied Randall. *"The two older brothers said, 'Yes indeed! You'll do it bravely, no doubt! You who have scarcely ever set your foot out of the door."*

"Bullies," said Taylor.

"Boots said nothing to this, but only begged them to give him a good store of food... That's not a store as in shop, but store as in supply, a good supply of food."

"Her."

"Pardon?"

"Boots begged them to give her a good supply of food."

"Right, her... *Her mother had no cheese, so she set the pot on the fire to make him...* her... *a little, and she...* that's Boots, not the mother... *put it into a scrip...* that's a carrying bag... *and set off."*

"Funny how the mother only shows up in the story when food needs to be prepared," said Taylor. Now she openly smiled. She sat up taller and rested her elbows on her knees.

"So when she had chopped a bit, the Troll came to her

and said, If you cut this forest of mine, I'll kill you. But the girl was not slow, she pulled her cheese out of her bag in a trice... that's fast... *and squeezed it till the whey spurted out."*

"Ew. Gross," said Taylor.

"Hold your tongue."

"What?"

"It's the story... *Hold your tongue, she cried to the Troll.* She wasn't crying, as in weeping, it means..."

"Yeah, I got it."

"Hold your tongue, she cried to the Troll, or I'll squeeze you as I squeezed the water out of this white stone."

"That's a lie," said Taylor.

"Not a lie, a trick."

"What's the difference?" asked Taylor, tilting her head and putting on an innocent expression.

"A lie is a deliberate misrepresentation of the truth, often to mask guilt. A trick is a deception to fool someone, often for amusement, or in this case as a sort of strategy."

"So, it's okay to lie?"

"That's not the point here. Boots is using his, I mean her, wits to outsmart the Troll."

"So she can steal his natural resources."

"The forest belongs to her father, who needs to sell it to pay off his debts."

"Perhaps her father should have been living within his means," said Taylor with a shrug of her shoulders.

"Let's get back to the story. *Nay dear friend! said the Troll...*"

"She's not his friend," mumbled Taylor.

Randall looked at Taylor over the top of his glasses and continued. *"Nay dear friend! said the Troll. Only spare me, and I'll help you chop."*

"So much for saving the environment." Taylor threw up her hands and let them fall to her sides.

"Well on those terms the lad... I mean lass... was willing to spare him, and the Troll chopped so bravely, that they felled and cut up many, many fathoms in the day."

"So now they're clear-cutting?"

"Taylor, can you stop interrupting and just enjoy the story?"

"Fine."

"But when evening drew near the Troll said, Now you'd better come home with me, for my house is nearer than yours."

"Uh-oh. I hope Boots has been taught about stranger danger."

"The lass was willing enough and when they reached the Troll's house..."

"Located in the forest, confirming his ownership of the property."

"...the Troll was to make up the fire, while the lass went to fetch water for their porridge. There stood two iron pails so big and heavy that she couldn't so much as lift them from the ground."

"Just as well. Porridge for dinner sounds nasty."

"Pooh! said the lass..."

"Really? The book says pooh?"

"Yes. You were going to listen without comment. Remember?"

"Fine."

"Pooh! said the lass. It isn't worthwhile to touch these finger basins. I'll just go and fetch the spring itself."

Taylor inhaled a deep breath and, when her father turned to look, she made a gesture as if zipping her mouth closed.

"Boots is unable to lift the heavy iron pots," explained Randall. "But she can't show weakness in front of the Troll so she is talking with bravado."

Taylor raised both eyebrows.

"Not a lie," said Randall, "another trick to manipulate the Troll."

Taylor made her eyes wide and looked up toward the ceiling while keeping her lips pressed together.

Randall shook his head and continued, *"Nay, nay, dear friend, said the Troll."* He ignored Taylor's snort. *"I can't afford to lose my spring, just make up the fire and I'll go and fetch the water. So when he came back with the water, they set to and boiled up a great pot of porridge."*

Taylor reached to her bedside table and turned the alarm clock face so she could see it.

"Almost done," said Randall. *"It's all the same to me, said the lass, but if you're of my mind, we'll eat a match!"* Randall noticed that Taylor was staring off into space. "She's challenging the Troll to an eating contest," he said. "I wonder who is going to win."

"I wonder," replied Taylor, rolling her eyes. "Ooops. Sorry." Then she zipped her mouth again.

"With all my heart, said the Troll, for he thought he could surely hold his own eating. So they sat down, but the lass took her bag unawares to the Troll, and hung it in front of

herself. She scooped more into the bag than she ate herself and when the bag was full, she took up her knife and made a slit in the bag."

"A liar and a cheat," said Taylor. She slumped down and folded her arms across her chest.

"The Troll looked on all the while, but said never a word. When they had eaten a good bit longer, the Troll laid down his spoon saying, Nay! but I can't eat a morsel more."

"But you shall eat, said the youth. I'm only half done. Why don't you do as I did and cut a hole in your paunch? You'll be able to eat as much as you please."

"What! She lies, cheats and now she's going to murder the Troll, who has done nothing more than protect his rightful property? What kinda kids' story is this?" asked Taylor. "Did you pre-read this to see if the content was suitable, father?"

"It's almost done."

"Fine."

"But doesn't it hurt one cruelly? asked the Troll. Oh, said the youth, nothing to speak of. So the Troll did as the lass said, and then you must know very well that he lost his life, but the lass took all the silver and gold she found in the hillside..."

"Murderer. Thief," grumbled Taylor.

"...and she went home with it, and you may fancy it went a great way to pay off the debt." Randall closed the book and placed it in his lap.

"That's it? That's the end?" asked Taylor as she ran her fingers through her hair. "Let me get this straight. The father is in debt, can't manage his own money, so he expects his children to dig him out of the hole he has created. The wife is no help, all she can do is make food. The father wants his kids to steal resources from an indigenous person, who they don't respect because he looks different than them and is uneducated. The sons try to do what they're told, but when the indigenous person tells them to get lost, their father mocks them, destroying their self-esteem. Then the daughter, who no one has any confidence in, resorts to lying, cheating, murder and theft in order to prove herself worthy of her father's love. The environment is wrecked and the rightful landowner murdered, but that's okay because the father's debts are paid so he can continue his irresponsible lifestyle."

"That's about it," said Randall. "Maybe tomorrow night you can read your story to me."

Septic Hot Tub

After a long, stressful day, the only thought that keeps Janice moving is the imagined delight of lowering herself into a soothing hot tub. She likes to be parboiled. The extra weight she carries with her all day floats, light as air, and her aging joints relish the pounding heat of the jets. If she conjures up the vision of immersing herself she can make it through the barrage of demands for her attention.

As she drives across town, Janice smiles at the athletic bag riding shotgun. She pictures herself shoulder-deep in a whirlpool of soothing liquid. Like a human teabag the stress of her day will seep from her tired carcass and she will be renewed.

In the crowded change room Janice retires to a private cubicle to put on her bathing suit. She has cut the size and brand tag from the back. No need to advertise for the plus-size chain store. She knows it's a scam when they equate her stature with being a queen. As she tugs the suit over her ample thighs, she checks for breaks in the seams. Thank God, the suit remains intact, and there's no need to subject herself to the dreaded task of buying a new one.

Janice notices a sign at the entrance to the shower area. It says that proper attire is required when using the pool. It clarifies the definition of proper attire as spandex clothing designed for swimming. Janice chuckles. Clearly her complaint has been acknowledged. Several weeks ago she entered the hot tub to find a woman sitting there in her underwear and bra. Not only had the water rendered them transparent, resulting in an over-sharing that burned the image into Janice's subconscious, but she also wondered whether the woman had brought fresh undergarments to swim in, or if these were the items she had worn all day and this was some kind of laundry ritual. She had only dared soak her feet that day.

Janice steps into the shower, lathers up and rinses off before entering the pool area. Out on the deck she heads towards her bubbling destination. She smiles when she sees there's only one person in the tub. It's so awkward when there's a crowd and people cannot help brushing against one another beneath the churning water. Today there will be room to stretch out, and enjoy multiple jets. As she studies the back of the occupant's head, Janice strategizes about the optimum location to avoid eye contact and unwanted conversation.

Before entering Janice adjusts the timer, resetting it to the 15 minute maximum. The timer had almost expired, so perhaps the current occupant is due to get out. *What an odd activity this is*, Janice thinks. *Bathing with strangers.* She envisions herself stepping into an ancient Roman spa. Janice tilts her chin up and steps into the water in what she imagines to be slow motion. She feels the heat slide up from her toes to caress her calves, thighs and…

Janice stifles a sigh of delight when she looks up to see the tub's other occupant. The woman is slumped in the corner, chin on her chest and eyes closed. For a moment Janice panics, thinking the woman is dead. Then her tub mate raises her head and meets Janice's gaze. "Tired…

after a long day?" Janice inquires, before lowering herself to the submerged bench.

"No… I'm sick," is the reply.

Janice shrieks internally. Suddenly the water seems to be a stew of incubating germs. She can see it as clearly as a specimen under a microscope. She rises to perch on the edge of the tub. Janice decides to wait out the occupant's departure.

"Got a touch of a cold?" Janice asks as she positions the sole of her left foot in front of a jet. "There are a lot of bugs going around."

"No. Food poisoning," the woman says. "I've had diarrhea all day. I think it was the Mexican food I had last night. That place on Jefferson Drive, avoid it."

"Oh dear, you poor thing. You probably just want to get home and collapse in bed," says Janice, switching her feet so the right sole is in front of the jet.

"You are so right. I've been here for 20 minutes. Time to drag my sorry ass home." The woman climbs out of the tub, wishes Janice a good evening and shuffles back to the change room.

Janice slides into the glorious warmth of the water. She tells herself food poisoning is not contagious and most certainly the woman had taken a shower before entering the tub. She slides down until her shoulders are under the water and positions herself with a jet at the base of her spine.

Recalling the ill woman's static pose Janice remembers how she had thought the woman was dead, or at least unconscious. She fantasizes about how she would rescue a person in that situation. She would drag the immobile woman to the pool deck. Janice had been a lifeguard during high school and clearly recalls the procedure to move someone into a recovery position. There is an emergency phone next to the tub timer. Janice imagines making the 911 call and how promptly the team of handsome firefighters would arrive. Of course they would commend her on her calm handling of the situation. Janice smirks as she pictures being photographed with the first responders. In her mind's eye she looks stunning in her suit.

Just as Janice is basking in the glow of her imagined heroism, two women arrive and head toward the hot tub. They are young, fit and are chatting animatedly as they cross the deck. They each wear a skimpy two-piece and both have their hair gathered in a messy bun. Janice panics. She begins coughing. The closer the two come, the louder Janice coughs. When she sees them pause, their gabbing interrupted, Janice makes a noise as if she is clearing phlegm from her throat. The bikini-clad babes do an about-face and make a hasty exit. Janice giggles.

Basking in the comfort of the bubbling water, Janice revises the heroic fantasy. She pictures a fireman draping her in a blanket as the ill woman is taken away on a stretcher. With his arm on Janice's shoulder the firefighter tells a cluster of reporters that Janice's quick thinking has saved the woman's life. Janice stretches out on the tub's bench, eyes closed and jets massaging the length of her Rubenesque figure. Had there been someone else present they would see her smile, and nod her head, as she imagines modestly accepting the media's praise.

Abruptly the fireman removes his arm from Janice's shoulder and the crowd of admirers disappears. She opens her eyes and sits upright. The jets have shut off. The timer has a 15-minute maximum. Janice decides to take advantage of her sole occupancy and step out to reset the timer. As she twists the dial… an alarm goes off.

"Shit!" She wonders whether the club installed the alarm to enforce the 15-minute maximum. She moves the dial backward to see if the ringing will stop.

The public address system clicks on. "Attention members. Please exit the building in an orderly manner. This is not a drill. Please exit the building promptly."

Janice dances on the spot as she scans the empty deck area. There is a fire exit to her right, which leads directly to the building's front parking lot. The change room door is at the far end of the deck and leads back into the heart of the building, which she imagines engulfed in flames. She grabs her towel from its hook, slips on her flip-flops and pushes on the exit door's crash bar.

A crowd is gathering in the parking lot. Janice tries to wrap the towel around herself but there isn't quite enough length to tuck it in, so she clutches it together at her chest. She spots her car and starts heading toward it, then realizes without her keys the car offers no sanctuary. She claims a position behind a group of women who had clearly been in a yoga class. They're clad in spandex leggings and had the presence of mind to rescue their colourful mats as they exited.

The sound of sirens approaches and Janice becomes frantic to find shelter. She steps between a row of parked cars. A large fire truck pulls up in front of the facility. Firefighters clad in long coats, rubber boots and hard hats enter the building. The evacuees are milling about, many socializing, some complaining they have not snagged their possessions on the way out and thus are unable to head home. Janice is starting to feel chilled in her damp suit and tiny towel. This is hardly the relaxing end to her day she had imagined. She sees a staff member talking to the yoga people and decides to step closer to hear the information being shared. To her surprise, as she approaches the group, a firefighter appears from behind the truck and places a soft blanket over her shoulders.

"You got caught by surprise, I see," says the handsome young man. "This will keep you warm. We wouldn't want you to get sick."

I'm Just A Girl

"Don't you want to look sophisticated and sexy?" Tiffany sighed as she spun the display rack of press-on gemstones. She nonchalantly checked the time on her phone. Less than 30 minutes and their mothers would be back. "Seriously, Amber, the reason our mothers throw us together is so I can teach you some style. Check it out." She handed Amber a package.

"I-I don't know," stammered Amber. "I just think that… well… wearing a jewel on your forehead means something. Doesn't it?" The smell of incense tickled her nose and started to give her a headache.

"That's what makes it fabulous," Tiffany replied as she started pulling cards of gemstones off the rack, tilting them to see how they caught the light from the overhead halogens. She handed another to Amber. "It, like, symbolizes the third eye. You know, like, that chalk-raw stuff. It's a meditation thingy."

"B-but, isn't it… I don't know… racist to use sacred stuff for fashion?" Amber read the back of the card. All that was written were the peel-n-stick instructions. The front of the card displayed a line drawing of a woman's face showing the placement of the gemstone between the eyebrows.

Tiffany held a package to her own forehead and inspected her reflection in the rack's mirror. She brushed her long blond hair behind her shoulders and noticed her blue eyeliner had worn off. "Nah. They wouldn't be allowed to sell it if it wasn't okay. It's just… beautiful. Don't ya think?" She modeled the package against her forehead for her companion. "It kinda looks Egyptian, like… ah, what's her name?"

"Cleopatra?" said Amber.

"Yeah. The Queen of the Damned."

"No, that's the movie. About the vampires, I think. Cleo—"

"Doesn't matter. It's sexy." Tiffany opened the package and tested the strength of the gem's adhesive with her finger. "I wonder if it would cause a zit."

"But… isn't it religious or something? I think people from India wear them."

"Are you kidding? The world is a global village, Amber. All kinds of foreign shit is really hot. I saw Gwen Stefani wearing one in her music video, you know… 'I'm Just a Girl'." Tiffany adhered a turquoise gem to the crease between her eyebrows, then tilted her head and admired herself in the mirror. She decided it matched the colour in her eyes perfectly.

Amber rubbed her nose in an attempt to stifle a sneeze, then pulled out her phone to Google the meaning of the forehead jewel. "It says here that it's called a bindi, which means dot."

Tiffany snorted. "Kinda obvious, doncha think?" She stuck the gem back on the card and slipped the package into her pocket.

"It's a sacred symbol of the universe… sometimes called the third eye… "

"Told ya."

"… and has historical and cultural significance in the

region of Greater India." Amber put her phone away. She followed her companion who pawed through a display of silk scarves. "Tiffany, don't you find it offensive when white people take something from another culture and market it as a fashion statement or status symbol?"

"You're a white person, Amber."

"I'm aware of that."

"What do you think of this one?" Tiffany wrapped a cerulean blue scarf around her neck. "Look how it makes my eyes pop."

"It's very nice," said Amber.

"Am I being culturally offensive if I buy this scarf?" asked Tiffany.

"Very funny."

"Wouldn't want to offend," Tiffany said. She continued to wear the scarf while she meandered through the store. "Anyway, the whole point of this store is to sell third world merchandise."

"Developing nations."

"What?"

"Third world is an offensive term. The politically correct reference is developing nations."

"What?"

"Mr. Windermere told us in Geography class that labeling a culture third suggests it's of lesser value than North America."

"Have you *seen* photos of India?" Tiffany starting picking up semiprecious, polished stones. Each bin had a label with the geological name and the symbolism associated with the rock. "You're way too serious, Amber. You need to chill."

Marion Reidel

Amber started sniffing and wiped moisture from the corner of her eye.

"Oh m'god, are you going to cry? You're such a wuss?"

"No. There's something in the air. It's irritating me." Amber used the hem of her T-shirt to wipe her eyes.

"Look at this! It's the stone you're named after." Tiffany held up a golden crystal. "It says here… *Amber has marvelous metaphysical properties for psychic protection. It is a powerful healer that gives the person who wears it a lovely sense of health and healing.* You need this." Tiffany dropped the stone down the front of her companion's T-shirt, causing it to lodge in her bra.

"What the hell?" whispered Amber.

"It balances emotions, clears the mind and releases negative energy. Just what you need." Tiffany started laughing so loudly the sales clerk approached.

"May I help you ladies find anything?"

"No, thanks. We're just killing time until our mothers are done at the spa next door. I might take this though," said Tiffany unwrapping the scarf and handing it to the clerk.

"Super. I'll keep it at the cash register for you."

When the clerk departed Amber growled, "You're such an idiot. How am I supposed to get that stone out of my bra?"

"It'll be easy when you get home. In the meantime, think of all the healing energy pressed right against your precious little heart.

No Satisfaction

Randall resists detonation. He wonders how the day-to-day ineptitude of those around him has not caused society to implode.

In the solitude of his office, Randall rips a page slightly as he circles errors with red ink. He taps his foot on the plastic carpet protector beneath his desk and chews on the end of his pen. He did not ask his secretary to *compose* the memo. He dictated every word, indicated paragraph breaks and the spelling of the recipients' names. Randall smacks his own forehead with the heel of his hand. He draws a voluptuous female form on his desk blotter, then proceeds to impale her head with arrows.

Randall understands the only reason Suzi Westerly got the secretarial job is because her sweaters are spray-painted on. Bob Roberts, from Human Resources, has been making up reasons to drop by Randall's office, asking for trivial information. Bob leans over Suzi while she taps her keyboard with bedazzled nails. Suzi's incessant giggling alerts Randall to Bob's arrival, which allows him to grab the phone and fake an important conversation.

A rap on his door snaps Randall back to reality. Suzi peeks around the edge. "Is it okay if I go for lunch now, Mr. Paulson? I thought I would, like, eat my lunch at the picnic table with the girls today. It's nice and sunny… oh darn it. I forgot to bring any sunscreen with me. Oh well, I guess I'll have to, like, sit under the tree. But then stuff falls off and, like, gets stuck in my hair. I suppose that's just Mother Nature. Right?" She giggles and pats her poofy orange hair.

"Go right ahead and take your break, Miss Westerly. I plan to adjourn myself. I've indicated a few edits on this correspondence, and if you would be so kind as to revise them after lunch, I will sign the corrected versions and they will be ready for this afternoon's post."

"Sure thing, boss," she chirps, then turns and prances away.

Randall deposits the documents on Miss Westerly's desk. He picks up her novelty stapler, shaped like a finger with a bright pink nail. As he heads to lunch he drops the stapler in a colleague's waste bin.

* * *

In the building's lobby Randall joins the line at the Perk-Up Café and mentally rehearses his order for *coffee, black, and a ham-and-Swiss on light rye with yellow mustard.* He prefers to communicate as concisely as possible with customer service personnel. The place is busier than usual and Randall can't avoid overhearing the orders of customers ahead of him.

"I need an extra-large latte. Make it non-fat and no-foam. Oh, use soymilk instead of dairy because I think I might be lactose intolerant. And, I want a double vanilla shot. No, make it a triple shot. That was *extra*-large," demands the customer at the head of the line. Randall assesses the middle-aged woman in fuchsia yoga pants and floral tunic top. He notices the glow of sweat on her brow and the semi-circles of moisture under her arms, and withdraws his handkerchief to dry his palms.

The next customer is gazing at the price list, slack-jawed and blank-faced. Randall focuses on his breathing exercises. In… one, two, three… out… one, two, three… as she struggles to make a decision. "Let's see, I'll have a… medium… half sweet… non-fat… caramel… Macchiato. For here." The woman concludes with intonation suggesting she's just discovered the cure for cancer.

Only two more people ahead of him. *Oh, Lord help me*, thinks Randall. *It's the metrosexual salesman from the eighth floor.* The man's designer suit is clearly custom tailored to hang perfectly on a toned frame created by countless hours spent under the supervision of a personal trainer. His hair is glued in place with sculpting gel, creating a smooth ebony curve that catches the light from the overhead halogens. With a repressed smirk, Randall envisions what would happen if he held a match to the back of his carefully coiffed head.

"Hello there Randall," the stylish salesman says, straightening his lapel. He turns to depart with his beverage, then asks, "Did you hear I've just been promoted to regional sales director?" He hands Randall a business card printed on heavy cardstock with embossed lettering.

"Congratulations, Jerry," Randall replies.

"It's nice to be acknowledged," says the salesman, then he turns and walks away.

Randall tears the business card into confetti and surreptitiously lets the pieces drift to the floor as he steps up to order.

* * *

For the last five years, Randall has been commuting on the municipal transit system. He breathes as infrequently as possible and tries to mentally diminish his body mass to avoid contact with other passengers. He feels the monetary savings are well worth the physical torture. As he descends into the depths of the station, the aroma of urine and decay assault his nostrils. He withdraws his pristine white handkerchief from his breast pocket to cover his face, as if to muffle a sneeze. He never touches the railings or turnstiles with his bare hands and sitting on the benches is unthinkable. Randall stands straight and stoic, six inches from the wall, staring straight ahead as he awaits the train.

Once in the crowded car, Randall positions himself adjacent to the opposite doorway. A large Hispanic man, smelling of tobacco and beer, steps into the space directly in front of Randall. A tattoo is visible on the right side of his neck; something vaguely floral with swoopy Victorian-style writing. Randall wonders what someone might choose to have written on his own neck, but resolutely looks elsewhere. As the train jostles, the man loses his footing and bumps Randall's arm with his elbow.

"I'm sorry. Are you okay?" asks the man.

"Yes indeed," Randall replies. "Think nothing of it."

"It seems these trains get more crowded every day. It's hard for anyone to maintain discrete personal space," says the stranger.

"Mmmm. Difficult," replies Randall as he turns to face the opposite direction.

* * *

The walk home from the subway takes five minutes. As Randall proceeds along the tree-lined sidewalk, he's startled by a ferocious mongrel that strains against a chain link fence, has to sidestep a skateboarder and is almost struck by his neighbour, Mrs. Gregory, driving her car into the back alley without looking. He runs this gauntlet daily and spends sleepless nights listening to the same dog howl. He smirks to himself as he imagines cleansing the world of annoyances, creating a sense of calm that would soothe his nerves and nourish his soul.

As he steps into the foyer of his home, Randall is greeted by a stench that makes his stomach churn. His wife, Beth, is cooking cabbage. Randall sets down his briefcase, stands still for a moment, lowers his shoulders and flexes his fingers. Beth's tomato sauce is heavily laced with garlic, so tomorrow he'll have an offensive case of intestinal gas. He checks the stack of mail on the console table. Bills... advertisements... political propaganda. Randall rubs the smooth texture of the refined paper between his fingertips.

Stepping into the kitchen, he is confronted by his twelve-year-old daughter. She is wearing an untucked checked shirt, striped capri pants and mismatched socks. Her drawings and craft projects cover the fridge and spatter the sliding glass door to the deck.

"Another meaningful day in the corporate world, father?"

He looks at Taylor's closely cropped hair and large blue eyes, then sets the mail on the kitchen counter without response.

His wife approaches holding a glass of red wine. Her voice grates on Randall like sand in bathing trunks.

"Hi Sweetie, did you have a good day? Want a cocktail?

Celeste called today. They just got back from their holiday. Sounds like they had a fabulous time. Such an exotic place. And they had so many adventures. I can't wait to see the photos. Charles had some stomach problems. Celeste warned him that using ice cubes is the same as drinking the tap water, but you know Charles. He always thinks he knows best. Apparently he had cramps so bad he couldn't get out of bed for a whole day. Still... their cabana was situated right on the beach and they had an all you can eat buffet... Did you want that drink, Honey?"

"No, thank you. I am going to change before dinner."

Randall hangs his suit carefully and changes into his only pair of jeans and a plaid shirt. He takes a wallet out of his dresser and slides it into his back pocket. As his wife and daughter begin their dinners, Randall indicates he will carry the compost out to the backyard container. They do not notice him take his jacket from the hook by the back door as he departs. After dropping the waste into the Green Machine Scrap Eater, Randall continues walking, out his back gate and down the alley that runs behind his house.

* * *

Beth is at a loss to explain why her husband has disappeared. She straightens the place mat in front of her as she watches the officer make entries in his notebook. "We didn't have an argument. I can't think of any conflict that would make him leave." She reaches for her warm tea and takes a sip despite its inability to offer comfort. She sets the cup down, aligns her place mat with the edge of the table and responds to the officer's inquiries. "He was wearing his jeans and favourite plaid shirt." She'd noticed this morning his jacket was gone. But his briefcase, the symbol of everything he valued, an engraved gift from his parents upon his graduation, is standing sentry in the hall exactly two inches out and perfectly parallel to the wall. She smooths the edges of her place mat. "No, an affair is unthinkable. There are no debt worries. I have no idea why he walked away."

While flipping his notebook shut, the interviewing officer exchanges a knowing look with his partner. They exit to the backyard, searching for signs of a struggle, then head down the alley.

The neighbour, Mrs. Gregory, peeks out the crack in her dining room curtain. She sees the police cruiser in the Paulson's driveway and when the officers begin searching the alley she scurries out to speak with them. When they ask if she'd seen Randall, she eagerly responds. "Why, I nearly hit him with my car on my way home yesterday. Then, around dinnertime, I saw him walking down this alley, like he had somewhere to go." She smiles as the officers takes notes. "He walks very quickly, you know. He literally jumped in front of my car on my way home from the grocery store."

She answers questions confidently. "No, I didn't see him carrying anything. Yes, I'm sure. No. He was alone. Yes. Of course I'm sure."

The police spend several weeks canvassing the neighbourhood and interrogating work colleagues, but discover nothing. With no evidence to suggest foul play and no financial trail to follow, they set the investigation aside and move on to more urgent issues.

* * *

Randall slips the unfamiliar currency into his pocket and heads from the *Banco Nacional* back to the beach. He considers how it took only four years to funnel sufficient company funds to his numbered account. *Amazing what a little rounding down will do.* Randall smirks.

The tropical breeze ruffles Randall's thinning hair while he tries to ignore the grit between the toes of his sandal-clad feet. He inhales the salty air and notices a hint of rotting seaweed or uncollected garbage; he's not sure which. As Randall takes his favourite seat at the bar of *El Iguanas* restaurant, he admires the view of the beach through the open walls. The ocean is jade, the same colour as the *Lagoon* paint Beth used for their en-suite bathroom. He admires his surroundings, but wonders how sanitary it is to have exotic birds hopping among the restaurant's tables. He shifts on his stool in response to bamboo poking his backside, then notices tourists at the other end of the bar.

"What do you mean you can't make an iced skinny mocha latte?" asks a woman so sunburnt she looks like she's about to have a stroke.

"See here, any decent Scotch selection should include a twelve-year-old single malt," declares her husband, who is wearing an oversized button-down shirt with a colourful tropical motif. "Do you make your ice cubes from bottled water?"

Randall hopes the bartender slips them both a nice little intestinal parasite as a souvenir of their vacation.

We Drank Wine

As they moved towards their 50th benchmark, Celeste made a habit of covertly evaluating her friends' sags and wrinkles to confirm she was aging more gracefully. Her professionally decorated home was larger, her husband much more successful, her children significantly more attractive, and her personal trainer berated her into fine athletic form. The countless squats gave her the butt of a twenty-year-old.

Celeste clicked her bright red, perfectly manicured nails on the table's glass surface, then leaned to the left and checked her reflection in the bistro's window. A gentle sweep of her palm directed stray hairs, the colour of wheat, to rejoin her French bun. With a tweak she untwisted her jade pendant earring and gave her head a little shake. Her teeth, recently whitened, shone like perfectly matched pearls framed by lips the same hue as her nails. Vintage frame sunglasses and a floppy hat gave Celeste an aura of mystery as she basked in the afternoon heat while awaiting her companion.

A waiter arrived with a carafe, topped-up her drink and set a second glass on the table. Celeste pondered how Sandy's life seemed to be falling apart. They'd been best friends since university, wed within a month of each other. But almost eighteen years later, Celeste and Charles were enjoying an affluent martial partnership, while Robert and Sandy's marriage shattered.

Celeste sipped her wine and scanned the café, hoping someone she knew might witness how put-together she looked. She spotted a neighbour's husband, with two other men in suits, situated at the opposite end of the al fresco dining space. She crossed her legs, repositioned her hemline and saluted with her glass when he glanced her way.

The metal chair to her left screeched on the patio stones as her hefty lunch date collapsed into the seat and deposited a shoulder bag beneath the table.

"Janice, darling, you're here." Celeste set her glass down and tapped her phone awake to check the time.

"Sorry. I left on time, but traffic was a nightmare. They've dug up Main Street from Westwood to Brant. I took the detour around the city centre but everyone else seemed to have the same idea, so we just crawled along. The darn air conditioning isn't working in the van so I had to have the window down and now my hair —"

"Really? Well, you're here now, Honey. I ordered Chardonnay. Let me pour you a drink." Her bangle bracelets were musical as Celeste filled her friend's glass to the brim. "So, what have you heard about Sandy and Robert?"

"I don't know. Sandy isn't up to talking." Janice dug through her oversized shoulder bag and extracted a wire brush. As she dragged it through her short frizzy hair crescents of perspiration were revealed beneath the armholes of her floral summer shift.

"But... didn't you go over there yesterday? I thought you had lunch with her?"

"I did. She seemed very upset. I spent most of the time making her a bowl of soup and telling her everything was going to be okay. I find people in mourning respond well to food. A hot bowl of chicken noodle cures just about anything. I took her some of my tollhouse cookies. No one can resist their chocolaty goodness."

"Janice! I need information. What did Sandy say… exactly?" Celeste removed her sunglasses, leaned in and absentmindedly resumed tapping her nails on the table.

"She really didn't give me details. You can't repeat this, Celeste. Okay?"

"Of course. Of course. I am asking out of concern. You know I'd never betray Sandy's privacy."

"Well, okay… two weeks ago Robert called her… from Toronto. He's been there overseeing some big project. I think it's a new shopping mall, or it could be a medical building. Whatever it is, he's been staying overnight rather than driving back and forth. You know they've been having issues for months."

"What kind of issues specifically?"

"Well, for one thing," Janice switched to a whisper, "they're sleeping in different bedrooms. He's staying in the master suite and she's moved into the guest room. I don't know how she manages without a walk-in closet. She has way too many clothes to —"

"How could you possibly know that, Janice?"

"Well, I've seen her closet Celeste."

"No. How do you know they're using separate bedrooms?"

"Oh. We've got the same housekeeper. You know Greta, the one who used to work for the Robinsons. When the Robinsons moved to Vancouver, because Al's company transferred him, Sandy snapped Greta up, but she couldn't afford her every week so we share. We each get her every second week. Sandy still cleans before Greta comes, you know how worried Sandy is about people judging her. Personally, I think she's crazy, but—"

"So… Robert and Sandy are sleeping in different bedrooms. That doesn't necessarily mean anything is wrong. Maybe he snores, or maybe she has restless leg syndrome."

"Oh no, it's much more serious. Sandy said when Robert called her from Toronto, well, he told her that, uh, he didn't love her anymore." Janice took a quick sip of wine and checked to see if anyone listening.

"Why didn't you say that when I first asked?" Celeste sat back in her chair and finished off her wine. She set down her glass and ran the nail of her index finger across her lower incisor as she watched Janice drink. "At this point in our lives love has *nothing* to do with making a marriage work."

"Robert told Sandy that he wants a… d-i-v-o-r-c-e."

"Don't be childish, Janice. It's not a dirty word. Lots of people get divorced. It's 'trending' as the kids say. What did he give as a reason? Does he have a mistress? Sandy said his new secretary has huge breasts and wears spiked heels."

"To work? That can't be very comfortable. Her legs would get very tired with all the walking back and forth to the –"

"Yes, to work. Where else? Focus, Janice." Celeste topped up her friend's glass, emptying the carafe. She signaled to a server with a snap of her polished fingertips, then resumed her engaged listener pose. "What else did she say?"

"Well… you'll never guess why Robert wants out of the marriage."

"I have no intention of guessing. Just tell me. Please."

"He's gay."

The waiter flinched as he stepped up to the table. "Will there be anything else, ladies?"

"The cheque," Celeste instructed with a wave of her hand. When the waiter had withdrawn she turned back to ask, "What do you mean, 'He's gay?' They've been married for 18 years."

"Apparently he didn't realize that he... preferred men." Janice glanced at the other patrons to check for eavesdroppers. "At first he was... you know... regular... but he had to... what's it called?... come out of the closet, because he became gay."

"Janice, darling, you are so naive. Okay, finish your wine. We need to go. I'll call Beth to tell her what's happening."

"Celeste, I don't think we should get in the middle of this. Sandy might not appreciate everyone knowing her personal business."

"What do you mean 'everyone'? I'm talking about just us girls. We've known each other since university, supported each other through the hell of childrearing, held Beth's hand when *her* husband left, and if you think for a second that I am going to abandon my best friend in the entire world when she needs me most, then you don't know me very well." Celeste picked up her purse and started to rise.

"I'm just saying that pushing ourselves on her might make it worse."

"Nonsense. Having her friends rally around her will give Sandy the strength she needs at this time. Drink your wine while I pay the bill and call Beth. We'll pick her up on our way over to Sandy's."

Celeste loved to have a mission. She'd been a member of the *Always Helping Others League* for two years and got tremendous satisfaction from fixing other people's problems and improving their quality of life. It was her calling.

* * *

Celeste led the trio's march up the steps to Sandy's suburban home. It struck her that the perfectly maintained yard, cheery blue shutters and welcoming arrangement of wicker porch furniture did not hint at the chaos huddled within. Keeping up appearances is so important.

Before knocking, Celeste smoothed her dress and withdrew a compact to check her face, then turned to evaluate her companions. Janice, her unruly mop of mousy brown curls tamed, and her body temperature settled so sweat no longer stained her dress. She wore an orange floral shift, more of a muumuu really, a tent-like style Janice felt hid the extra weight she carried. Her posture tilted due to the large satchel hanging on her left shoulder. "Do stand up, Janice. We want to look strong and confident for Sandy, not slumpy and depressed. That won't help her."

Celeste had hurried Beth to join the mission. There were tiny pills on the fabric of the peach top Beth wore. She had matching capris that were a man-made fibre with an elastic waist. Celeste wondered how Beth could tolerate the feel of it. Beth's petite frame was topped by dyed burgundy hair gelled into spikes that were meant to look youthful. Someday Celeste planned to take Beth for a makeover, but today's mission focused on Sandy. "Okay ladies, you know what we need to do, right? Sandy needs us and we will be strong for her." Celeste rapped on the door.

"Oh, hi guys. What are you doing here?" said Sandy. Although she did not open the door fully, Celeste could see that she wore one of Devon's hoodies over her pajamas and had not brushed her hair or put on makeup.

"We've come to support you." Celeste stepped forward, causing Sandy to stand aside and open the door completely. Janice and Beth offered cheery greetings as they followed their leader into the kitchen.

Celeste evaluated the disaster. Dishes in the sink, a greasy frying pan on the stove, two open wine bottles on the counter and a half-filled glass on the table. "Don't worry, we're here for you." Celeste took a seat at the head of the table. Janice and Beth sat on either side of her leaving the chair with the wineglass for Sandy. "We are aware of your situation. What do you need us to do?" asked Celeste.

"Nothing," said Sandy as she eased into her chair and began playing with the stem of her glass.

"I can't believe this has happened to you," said Janice, taking Sandy's hand in her own. "It is so unfair. You've been a dedicated wife... and mother. How could Robert be so selfish? You don't deserve this."

"That's not helpful, Janice," said Celeste. "Let's not even talk about Robert. Sandy is our concern."

"I'm fine," said Sandy, gently withdrawing her hand from Janice's grasp. She let her gaze fall on her own hands. She had an unreadable expression.

"No. Clearly you're not fine," countered Celeste. "Look at this place. I can see you're not functioning. And you're drinking wine. It's only... one o'clock in the afternoon. How many glasses have you had?"

"Celeste, but *we* just –"

"I'm not speaking to you, Janice." Celeste reached for Sandy's glass. "Alcohol is not going to fix your situation."

Sandy drew her wine closer, and held a neutral expression. "I'm fine."

"I know what it's like to be abandoned," offered Beth. "When Randall left I didn't know how I'd cope. It was so unexpected. If it wasn't for you guys, taking Taylor and telling me I'm still worthy of love, I think I'd have killed myself."

"That's not helpful, Beth. The goal here is to keep Sandy from getting depressed. By the way, where *are* Amber and Devon?"

"At my mother's."

"Do they know what's going on?" asked Celeste.

"I don't even know what's going on," sighed Sandy.

"Talk to me," said Celeste.

"First, I need to refill my glass," said Sandy, rising from the table. "Can I pour for anyone else?"

"No, we're fine," replied Celeste with a quick glance to her two companions. "Perhaps you'd be better with a big glass of filtered water, Sweetie?"

Sandy turned from the counter holding the bottle in one hand and the smudged glass in the other. "I'm okay."

"It's just… I notice your recycling bin is full of empties. I am concerned about your well-being," said Celeste.

"I'm okay."

"Drinking can easily get out of control if you're not careful," said Celeste.

"My cousin had a drinking problem. She kept it hidden for years," Janice chimed in. "Then one day she drove her car into the back of a garbage truck. The police took her license away, which meant she couldn't get to work. So, she lost her job, and her husband wanted her to go to rehab, but… they couldn't afford it, so she had to—"

"All right Janice. Sandy knows we're concerned." Celeste observed Sandy, frozen in position, leaning against the kitchen counter, bottle and glass still suspended in front of her.

"We love you so much," said Beth. "I know how painful it is to feel abandoned. I've walked in your shoes. Please let us help."

"I'm okay," said Sandy as she filled the glass, returned to her seat and set the bottle on the table.

An awkward pause crept into the room, sidling up to the table and casting a chill over the companions. Eye contact became difficult to sustain. The only sound in the room was the wall clock's ticking and the hum of the refrigerator. A car drove down the street and children's laughter could be heard in an adjacent yard. Sandy took a sip of her wine and asked, "What is it you guys want?"

"We want to help you," said Celeste.

"I'm okay."

"You're absolutely not," declared Celeste. "Your husband of 18 years has suddenly told you he's not who you thought you knew. You probably feel like your life has been a charade. At forty-five you're facing the prospect of being a single parent of two adolescents and the unlikely chance of finding another life partner. And now, it's clear you've taken up self-medicating, with a very fine Merlot, and all we want to do is support you through this crisis."

"I'm okay. I don't need your help."

"Saying you're okay doesn't make it true," said Celeste.

"You can be honest with us," added Beth. "We're your friends. We love you. Nothing will ever change that."

"We're not here to judge you," said Celeste. "When Randall took off, nobody suggested Beth held any responsibility for the boredom or discontent that undoubtedly drove him to abandon his mundane life. It would never occur to us that Robert's homosexuality is based in your inability to meet his needs, or your appeal as a woman. We are here to support to you. Drinking is not going to make you better. Talk to us."

"You want me to talk to you? You're concerned about my drinking? Okay, hear this. I drank wine in university, with Robert, as he seduced me into loving him. He used to keep real glass goblets in the glove compartment of his broken-down M.G.B. We would drive out to the city limits, then spread a blanket in a field to make love... and drink wine."

Sandy took a deep breath before continuing. "I drank wine at my wedding. You two were there to witness the white dress and tiered cake. We drank pink champagne in tall flutes and the bubbles tickled my nose. We all got a little tipsy. I felt like I was could float on air, as I... drank wine." She lifted her glass.

"I drank wine with all of you," recalled Sandy, "when we had preschool children, and were desperate for adult conversation. We'd meet every Monday morning, in Celeste's living room and while the kids played we talked about the challenges and frustrations of parenting, while we drank wine."

She turned to her left. "I drank wine when you were brokenhearted, Beth. The man you loved, no longer loved you. Without a word he had walked away from his respectable life, leaving you crying and trying to cope. So… you and I drank wine."

Sandy shifted in the opposite direction. "I drank wine with you Janice, when Angela got pregnant and ran off with that ne'er-do-well, taking your only hope for a grandchild with her. When you thought your reason for living had gone, together we drank wine."

Looking directly across the table she continued, "I drank wine with you Celeste, when you worried your life was a trap. You were drowning in an endless routine of keeping up appearances and meeting the needs of others while your sense of self… evaporated. We took inventory of your situation, practiced gratitude and self-love, as we… drank… wine."

Sandy pushed her chair back from the table and began to gesture. "I drank mulled wine at neighbourhood pot-lucks. I drank wine at memorials for lost loved ones. I drank wine at country club festivities. I drank wine on girls' getaway weekends. I drank wine to celebrate and I drank wine to mourn. And, as I did this… each one of you also held a glass in your hand. So, who the hell are you to be judging me now?"

Celeste looked her friend straight in the eye, then asked, "Can you get three more glasses?"

Marion Reidel

Therapy

"I came because my lawyer said to, but that doesn't mean I need to participate." *Let touchy-feely counselor girl chew on that for a minute.* "My lawyer said he'll be satisfied if I am present and listen." *I'll just sit here and smile; that fulfills my obligation.*

Look at her gypsy skirt, hoop earrings and bangle bracelets. Who's she trying to fool. She isn't even old enough to be a child of the sixties. And her tone of voice... can't Robert hear how condescending she sounds? Listen to her blather.

"We all have masculine and feminine sides... on a continuum. It is the balance of life's Yin Yang that will determine who we are. How our essence will be expressed."

I can't believe this. What happened to my husband? This is real life, buddy. Pick a side. All this navel gazing, I can't find my authentic self, introspective bullshit. Why can't he suck it up and get on with his responsibilities?

Oh, here we go, let's hear his sob story. His father expected too much of him. Needed a successor to the family fortune. Robert Wells Jr., heir to the Wells Construction empire. Poor baby, only given tools and trucks to play with as a child? Such abuse. Am I expected to believe he wanted to play with Barbies?

Smile nicely. "No, thank-you. I have no response." *Thanks anyway, Gypsy Princess. I have plenty of insights, but I'll keep them to myself.*

"It sounds like you were required to conform to strict religious standards, Robert."

How would she know?

"Your parents seem to have had a narrow concept of gender identity."

Really? Forced participation in... sports. Abused through soccer and hockey. Where was children's aid? Any sexual interference from coaches... scout leaders? How is it I've known this man for over 20 years and this is the first I've heard of this?

Hmmm? Gypsy Princess wants to know if I have a question? Just smile. Hands held neatly in my lap to ensure they do not leap to Robert's throat.

"Can you elaborate on what your adolescent life was like, Robert?"

Oh yes, by all means. Have him describe the estate home his parents made him live in, with the yard that held a pool and tennis court. Have him describe the private school he attended, the summer camp they made him go to. Don't forget those trips to England, France and Italy, the music lessons, the car.

The Gypsy Princess can't get enough of this crap. Look at her handing Robert a tissue and stroking his forearm. Hands off, lady. He's still mine at this point, broken as he is. I've got the paperwork and I've not yet decided to cut him loose.

"Family pressures, societal expectations and religious doctrine can combine to cause one to deny one's true self, Robert."

Well, isn't that good to know. He didn't lie to the world, he lied to himself, she says. Couldn't face the shame. Ha! Poor thing. Explain to his kids for me, will ya?

"How do you feel, Sandra?"

Oh, oh. A direct question to me, tricky.

"Do you feel betrayed by Robert?"

A single raised eyebrow and close-lipped smile is my response. Hands still in my lap. What do you think, Princess?

"Can you understand Robert's perspective, Sandra? Are you able to place yourself in his position? Can you see that Robert has faced a life of overwhelming deceit? Is it clear to you he did not maliciously intend to misrepresent himself to you?"

No, no, no and no.

"He has acknowledged the pain he has caused you."

Really? He thinks I might feel some pain and turmoil as a result of his stepping out of the closet? So nice of him to notice others have been impacted.

What I'd like to know is why he kept the charade up at university. Explain that to me. He'd managed to ditch his jock strap when I met him in the drama club. Why couldn't he confine his acting to the stage instead of bringing it into our relationship? He's the one took me to bed. He's the one who suggested we get married. He's the one who decided we should have kids. What script was he working from? Tell me that, Princess! Smile. Nope. No questions. Just smile... relax... breathe.

"How's your relationship with your children, Robert?"

Okay, he's telling the truth now. He's a good father. He loves those kids more than anything in this world. He'd do anything for them, but... Why does he think Amber is 20 pounds overweight? What does he suppose triggered her comfort-eating? Not yet sixteen years old and her self-esteem is in the Dumpster. And can he explain why Devon has been forced to play hockey? Is Robert afraid his moody son will follow too closely in his footsteps? Hmm?

"Our goal today is to clear the air and identify how to move forward with your relationship. In the aftermath of Robert's awakening, you two still need to co-parent. An open line of communication is essential. Robert's newly discovered sexuality must not become a barrier."

It's not being gay that's the problem here, Princess. It's the lying, the deception. If my baby boy were to determine that he's homosexual it would be fine with me. As long as he doesn't marry some unsuspecting girl, get her pregnant and then fuck up her life by revealing he prefers men decades later.

"I think you've been very forthcoming, Robert. Sandra, I'm concerned by your inability to express your feelings. Surely you must have questions or concerns about what lies ahead for you and Robert."

Smile. Keep smiling. What am I supposed to do now? I've been married to Robert for 18 years. My prime is done and gone. How am I supposed to find someone else to spend the remainder of my life with? I've got a middle-aged body, and two kids with a gay father. Who's going to want a piece of this hot mess?

"Well, we've made a start at seeking resolution. Let me check my calendar… would Wednesdays, at 2:00 work for our ongoing sessions?"

Hmm? I wasn't listening. Nope. Not a chance in hell of me coming back here. Smiling. Still sitting perfectly upright. I'm fine. Let's finish this.

"Family counseling is a positive process to help the two

of you, as well as Amber and Devon, get through Robert's transition. We can even include the grandparents if that's helpful."

Ha! Joke's on you, Princess. I'm here because my lawyer told me to demonstrate I've tried to reconcile before I proceed to sue for divorce and take a great big chunk of the Wells Empire. We won't be expanding this reality theatre to include the children and grandparents, thanks. My father must never be in the same room as Robert again. And his mother has taken up drinking in a serious way. Says it's a good thing Robert's father died of a heart attack last year because this would have killed him. The kids are confused enough. Just leave them out of this.

"Sandra, it's difficult to proceed if you refuse to interact. Sandra? Are you listening to me? Sandra? Okay then. I will pencil in the Wednesday appointments and you two can give some thought to how you'd like to proceed. Thank you for your time today, Robert. I think you've made a really good start."

Look at him. At 46 years old Robert's perfect. He runs on a treadmill every bloody day. There's not an ounce of fat on him. He's in the sun so much he's got the bronzed, weathered look of a surfer. I should have been suspicious when he grew that George Michael almost-beard. And how come his grey is only coming in at the temples? Men get better looking with age, while women just sag.

"You've been very brave, Robert. It is not easy to reinvent one's self at midlife. Well done. So, you and Jerry have a condo in the city…"

He's brave? How am I supposed to find someone else?

Who's going to want me? I don't know any single men. None of my friends' husbands are worth stealing. Oh God, please God, don't make me do online dating. I'd die. Celibacy is the only solution. I'll just quietly shrivel up while Robert goes off and has the time of his life.

"Hey, don't worry about it. Here's a tissue. It's a very emotional time for everyone."

Now he's weeping again. God! I have worked hard to build a good life. I've made us a wonderful home, in the desirable neighbourhood. I've volunteered at the kids' school, and served on the hospital board... even got us invited to join the country club. I'm the one who built our circle of friends, even Celeste and Charles who we've known since university, were my friends first. He can't have our friends. If he wants a new life he can go find new friends. Get the hell out of town.

"The important thing is going to be keeping the lines of communication open. Next time we'll deal with how to talk to your kids... even if they are... unable to join us.

The kids are mine. The house is mine. I'm keeping the car, the club membership and the cottage. If he wants to walk away, he can walk away from it all. Don't look back, Robert. This is not a decision you can undo.

"Are you ready to go Sandra? Or is there something I can help you with?"

Shit! I hadn't realized that I've been gripping so tightly my nails have dug notches in the back of my hands. I haven't eaten a proper meal in a week and my recycling bin is loaded with empty bottles. I'll have to sneak them out a few at a time or the neighbours will gossip. I think I'm losing my mind.

"You know, Sandra, you and I can book a private session

if that would be better for you."

Smile. No thanks. I guess I'd better find myself my own Gypsy Girl. Only I'll make mine a Gypsy Boy. Yeah, some smooth-talking, swarthy type who'll tell me I am still desirable and none of this is my fault. I still deserve to be loved.

Okay, get me out of here. I was promised I only needed to do this once.

"Just to be clear, Sandra, you agreed Robert can come by the house tomorrow to gather up the rest of his clothing."

Smile and nod. More room in the closet for me. 'Cause he's out of the closet. Get it? Pathetic. I'm pathetic.

Keep breathing Sandy. Don't fall apart yet, not 'til you're safely in your car. My perfect life is gone, but it was never real in the first place. There's no going back. I'm done. I'll report that this meeting went very well indeed and my lawyer can get the paperwork started. Robert's not the only one with acting skills.

Marion Reidel

Amber Alert

Ti da ti, Ti da ti, Tum-tum
Ti da ti, Ti da ti, Tum-tum

I crack open one eye, slip my hand from under the warmth of the covers and grope for the cell phone on my bedside table.

Ti da ti, Ti da ti, Tum-tum
Ti da ti, Ti da ti, Tum-tum

I press "dismiss" as the *Good Morning Alarm* announces the onset of another day. I always wake-up jonesing for digital contact, so I pull the phone under my covers and let my thumbs dance across the screen. Honestly, I can feel my body begin to tingle with life as I discover 17 unread text messages, 10 tweets and a dozen Facebook updates. If only I didn't need to sleep. It makes my stomach lurch to think of the drama I miss while obliviously unconscious. I wish I didn't have to leave this lovely cocoon.

A few taps reveal what I expect. Myles was still on a rant about his algebra mark. An 87% is not good enough to get him into the engineering program his parents want. Ms. Barker is such a bitch. She acts like questions are a personal insult and mocks anyone who doesn't grasp concepts as she races through them. Myles works his ass off in that class. His dad even hired a tutor and he still can't break into the top percentile.

Emily spent the night throwing up again. At five-seven and 110 pounds, she sees herself as a hippopotamus. At school she eats nothing but raw vegetables, but Em's mother always forces her to consume pasta dripping in rich sauce for dinner. "Keep it down until I reach the can," Em always says. She can force food back up with a flick of her finger. Her mother doesn't have a clue.

"Amber… You up yet?" My mother is a fan of yelling; too lazy to walk upstairs.

I set my phone back on the nightstand and swing my feet to the floor with a groan. My room plays host to a perpetual draft that creeps along the floorboards in a direct line from the window to the closet beside my bed. I begin each morning with a stretch, then a shiver, before tiptoeing to my dresser to find something clean to wear.

I admire Emily's determination, but can't take that kind of control over my own life. I gave up worrying about my weight long ago. Comfort eating is my drug of choice. And besides, big girls are featured in a lot of music videos these days. If boys want some booty, then Amber Wells has the goods.

I pull on my favourite sweatpants and my faded "Water Is Life" t-shirt, then pick up my phone to check the third thread of texts. Bonnie, the final member of our foursome, has been ricocheting between rage and depression for the last two weeks. Her texts are focused and clear: "i want 2 kill that slut" "i hope her bleeched hair falls out" "im going to kill myself". Standard Bonnie drama.

Breakfast with my family is painful. Mother flounces around the kitchen fussing and faking enthusiasm for life.

It grates on my nerves like a cartoon soundtrack. Father left us two years ago. He has a boyfriend now and lives in a city condo. I like having access to a city centre crash pad and the guilt gifts that result from divorced parents, but visiting my father is uber awkward.

My brother, Devon, hasn't spoken in over a year, or at least it seems that way. When he hit puberty, his face erupted into a minefield of zits and his hormones triggered tantrums that would put a two-year-old to shame. He slouches at the kitchen table, a black hoodie obscuring his tormented face, shoveling brightly coloured, sugary cereal into his mouth with a tablespoon.

"Put that darn phone away and finish your breakfast," my mother commands as she places a glass of orange juice in front of me. Devon prefers Coke for breakfast, like he's fueling the acne that has become the core of his identity.

I wave my mother off. "I just need to remind Bonnie about our Biology test this morning." I type, "todds a toad. not worthy of you. piss on him."

In reality, Todd the superjock with the face of an angel, isn't interested in Bonnie. She's been idolizing him from across the cafeteria; going on and on about those big brown eyes and luscious lashes. Todd doesn't even know Bonnie exists, so it's no big surprise to me that Miss Captain of the Cheerleaders added Todd to her key chain. Still, Bonnie thinks the bitch stole Todd from her and it's my duty to back my buddy up.

*   *   *

There's no cell service on the stupid school bus. Something about the metal shell of that yellow tin can screws up the signal. I'm desperate for another digital hit by the time I disembark. There's a flurry of incoming messages from Myles and Em, as well as a long one from Bonnie. As I scan the threads I get a sour taste in my mouth and a stabbing pain in my temple. Something's up. Bonnie's anger is off the chart.

I have a fleeting thought about stopping by Guidance to ask Miss G. for assistance. She's chill and Bonnie would listen to her, but as soon as I step into the building Myles grabs my arm and drags me towards Bonnie's locker. He tells me, "She's really lost it this time. She's talking about punching Christi in the face and I think she's serious."

I mutter words of assurance to Myles as we push through the crowded hallway towards Bonnie's locker. Em's already there. "There's no fuckin' way I'm gonna let you assault that bitch," says Em. "She's not worth getting expelled over. Forget jerk face jock. You can do soooooo much better."

The first period warning bell rings, but talking Bonnie down off the ledge takes precedence. We head down the back staircase. There's a little space at the bottom, behind the stairs, where we can sit without anyone seeing us. We often eat out lunches there rather than in the caf. We devise a plan.

"Okay, breathe," I begin. "I get that you're pissed, but… you need to make sure you don't do something that screws up your life while entertaining your enemies. You know what I mean? If you go ape shit, you'll be the joke of the whole school. We don't want that."

Myles chimes in, "The Roman Emperor Marcus Aurelius once said, 'The best revenge is to be unlike him who performed the injury.' You are better than Christi and Todd. Don't lower yourself to their level."

Bonnie is in a world of her own. "I was thinking of something like the prom scene in 'Carrie.' Maybe I could drop a bucket of pig's blood on Christi in the cafeteria. Then set the whole place on fire."

"Sure, that's very reasonable." Em snorts and rolls her eyes.

"Okay, then… I'll challenge her to a fight. Like Inigo Montoya in 'The Princess Bride.' My name is Bonnie Birdwell. You stole my boyfriend. Prepare to die."

"I love that movie." Myles sighs.

"Amber, tell her she can't beat up Christi. She'll listen to you." Em pokes me with her elbow.

"Well, you probably *can* beat up Christi… but you shouldn't." I'm sitting next to Bonnie with our backs against the wall. I put my arm around her shoulder and she leans in to me. A good sign. "We all hate Christi. She's too fucking perfect to tolerate. She's never had a zit, her hair is straight and silky, she's a size fucking two, and her daddy's rich as… as…"

"Rich as fuck… That's what Lil Wayne'd say," suggests Em.

We laugh. Another good sign.

"Didn't you learn anything from studying 'Romeo and Juliet'?" asks Myles. "It's folly to pursue revenge. Nothing good ever comes of it."

"But it's fun to fanaticize about it," I suggest. "Let's get this out of your system. If we *could* take revenge, what would it look like?"

"I like revenge porn," says Em. "Get some pics of Christi blowing Todd and post them on the school's Twitter feed."

"Shaming is good," agrees Bonnie. "We could pick the threads out of the backside of her Cheerleading uniform. Then in front of the whole gym her thong embedded ass would hang out for all to see."

"Don't forget Todd," says Myles. "He must not go un-scathed. I think a special chocolate dessert for him. We'd make it with a whack of laxatives and have Dewy on the caf-eteria crew ensure only Todd got it. He'd be filling his pants by the middle of third period."

We continue to brainstorm for almost half an hour. We know our outrageous ideas will never be acted upon, but the therapeutic impact of voicing them is indisputable. I laugh so hard tears run down my cheeks.

"Listen, I can't afford to miss second period, so we need to wrap this thing up." I give Bonnie another hug. "Myles was right in the beginning. The best revenge is to demon-strate you're better than them. To hell with Todd and Christi. They deserve each other. We'll find you a real boyfriend. Someone with a sense of humour, is drop dead gorgeous, and has some creative talent –"

"Not a jock," adds Em.

"There are some great guys in the band," suggests Myl-es. "Duncan Watson has the dreamiest brown eyes, Dwanye Scofield has shoulders as wide as a doorway and Simon Bradfield has curls to die for."

Alpha Male

Devon secretly slipped a piece of mint gum into his mouth. Sliding the strip back with his tongue, he bit down on the soft surface, clenching his jaw. He continued to bite and release as he listened to the principal's rant about the need for improved maturity, a keener sense of responsibility and the limited potential for his future. Like internal armor, the gum occupied his mouth, blocking the defiant responses that fought to escape his tortured mind.

Returning to the outer office bench while parental contact was made, Devon prayed his mother would be out at one of her social commitments. Better to have his father summoned. His father's abandonment guilt guaranteed that he would help conspire to conceal this event. Devon's dad's eagerness to buy his son's love would be a get-out-of-jail-free card.

Blake slouched on the bench beside Devon. They called themselves *twin brothers of single mothers.* Catchy. Devon's father had left to pursue his midlife gender crisis; Blake's dad had been killed in a drunk driving accident that resulted in jail time for Blake's mother. Now he lived with his grandma. The boys found each other through their mutual lack of social status.

Both boys were tall and slim, with pale complexions and a curtain of carefully sculpted hair obscuring their faces. Their baggy jeans and black hoodies, the uniform of the disenfranchised, earned them the title of "black hoodie boys."

They crafted their identity to claim their place in the competitive high school culture. They were known, yet invisible at the same time.

The vice principal paused at their bench to pass comment. His pale blue jacket, unable to button across his massive stomach, flapped as he walked. A stain marked his pinstriped shirt, probably coffee, and a button had gone missing just above his belt line. Unable to resist the opportunity for sarcasm, the VP asked if they were having a nice day, laughed at his own wit, winked at the secretary, then closed his office door behind him.

The incident that brought the boys to the office had been inevitable. Andrew could not be called an innocent victim. He loved the spotlight. Andrew always expected his groupies to lick his high-tops. He invited the attention of others to feed his ego, then acted nonchalant, as if unaware of his status. Devon had not been taken in.

In the cafeteria that morning, Andrew's pack of elite adolescents had reminded Devon of a Warner Brothers cartoon. Andrew was clearly the alpha. He waited in line, wearing a backwards ball cap and baggy clothes. Loose fabric covered his athletic body to create an exaggerated presence. His burgundy sweatshirt, clearly new and expensive, bore an embroidered logo from a wilderness outfitter. Saggy grey sweatpants hung on his hips as he struck a casual pose, oblivious to those watching him.

With an exaggerated laugh, Andrew remarked on the progress of his sideburns. Facial hair was a phenomenon yet to be experienced by the Beta Boys clustered within Andrew's personal space. One boy gave a gentle stroke to his idol's cheek, delicately tracing a trail from the dark hairline to a strong jaw. The younger boy expressed enthusiastic admiration and sought Andrew's acknowledgement. That's when the image of the Warner Brother's classic "Chester and Spike" struck Devon. In the cartoon Spike, the bulldog, wears a red turtleneck sweater and bowler hat. He casually chews on a toothpick as he trots along, and the little mongrel Chester bounces around him saying, "Hey Spike, you want I should dig up some bones for ya? Anything you say, Spike. 'Cause you and me is pals. That's right, ain't it, Spike? Hey Spike, you wanna play ball? You wanna play ball? Huh Spike, you wanna? Huh? Huh? Huh? Huh Spike, you wanna?"

The Beta Boys' admiration seemed so pure and intense that the potential embarrassment of being observed had been forgotten. Their alpha held his physical space with the un-wavering confidence of inexperienced youth. Andrew's entourage remained fixed within his orbit by a magnet-ic personality, and reflected positive energy to recharge Andrew's self-esteem.

Blake suggested igniting Andrew's hair, a carefully sculpted bedhead, that contained enough alcohol-based gel to transform Andrew into a human torch. Devon enjoyed the mental image, but imposed restraint on his clone.

Devon observed a lone female standing apart from Andrew's pack. She kept a discreet distance, as she passively followed their conversation. A tight T-shirt and micro cutoff shorts hugged her bony frame. The girl's uniformly blond hair, fried by chemical intervention, was gathered in a pony tail. She had become a symphony of projecting edges. Her jaw, collarbone, shoulder blades, elbows, hips, knees, then ankles, served as protective spikes. The matchstick legs supporting her were covered in wounds. Insect bites had been absent-mindedly scratched until they bled, creating a map of her anxiety.

Devon knew her. Cassie Westerlake. They were in the same art class and she had serious drawing skills. Once she complimented Devon on his sketches. His journal housed action figures, vintage style heroes, done in felt-tip pen. Cassie Westerlake knew Devon's name, acknowledged his existence and, as a result, inhabited his dreams.

The principal interrupted Devon's thoughts. "I contacted your father, Devon. He's on his way. As for you, Blake, your grandma is feeling quite understandably frustrated. She's not up to coming in, so I explained the situation to her over the phone. She asked me to have Devon's father bring you home." He sighed, rubbed the bald dome of his head, looked at the boys like they had personally disappointed him, then returned to his office.

"I don't know why he's so pissed," hissed Blake. "It coulda been a lot worse. We didn't do nothin' really."

"Shut up," mumbled Devon. He slumped lower on the bench. The clatter of nails on keyboards, the buzz of the fluorescent lights, the subdued chatter of the secretaries created a hypnotizing white noise causing him to close his eyes.

"I'm just sayin'," continued Blake. "If we're going to get expelled anyway, we shoulda just torched the bastard. Andrew fucking Hardwick asked for it."

"Shut up, Blake." Devon let out a sigh of exhaustion.

"You know I'm right. Hardwick… hard dick. Thinks he's hot shit. Needs to be taken down a notch. Just sayin'." Blake checked for Devon's response, but his buddy's hoodie hung down over his eyes and Devon appeared to be asleep. "It was just a bump on the head. An ambulance ride is no big deal." When Devon did not respond he grumbled, "Just sayin'... coulda been worse." Blake absentmindedly started bouncing his right leg. He focused on chewing his already gnawed nails, spitting bits of himself on the office floor.

Behind closed lids Devon replayed the incident. Andrew had been in the cafeteria line, with his Beta Boys publicly stroking his ego and drooling their adoration. The usual scene. Cassie was the new factor. From where Devon sat, he could see the longing in her eyes as she watched Alpha Andrew dole out attention to his entourage.

He had wondered why a wonderful, sensitive, quirky girl like Cassie would be interested, but apparently Andrew's magnetism defies explanation. When Andrew turned in Cassie's direction, Devon had seen her lips part, preparing to speak to the adolescent god. Before she could utter a word, Andrew attacked, totally unprovoked.

Andrew looked Cassie up and down. The distasteful sneer on his face made it clear that her bony frame, covered with scabs and freckles and topped with straw, did not meet with his approval. She should've walked away. The imminent rejection was obvious. Andrew wouldn't be able to ignore her fragility.

Unfortunately for her, Cassie spoke. Devon would've given anything to have Cassie's attention. He fantasized about intimate conversations with her. Cassie could see Devon. She knew his name, admired his art... so why had he been overlooked, again?

His only vivid memory of the event was the physical sensation of his blood rising to his cheeks, and his fingers twitching. The situation escalated so fast Devon struggled to put events in sequence. Cassie said something to Andrew, maybe "Hello," or simply "Hi," some meek greeting. It seemed as if she pushed a detonation button on Andrew's forehead.

Andrew flushed... glanced around to see if anyone thought he'd encouraged Cassie's interest. Then, he spewed venom at her, like the blaze of a flamethrower, each blow amplified by the fuel of Beta adoration. "What are you looking at, hag? Don't talk to me, you anorexic leper. Get your scabby bag of bones out of my sight, you flat-chested lesbo. Seriously, it's lunchtime and you're making me gag." Andrew's followers echoed his laughter.

Devon could recall every syllable of Andrew's insults, but the flash of anger that catapulted Devon from his chair created a white void. Somehow he transported from being a seated observer to standing face-to-face with Andrew. With their chests nearly touching, Devon had a height advantage, but Andrew had the muscle mass. Devon knew he spoke to Andrew, but the words eluded him. Some bystander would fill in the blanks.

The tension in his clenched fists, his locked jaw, staring into Andrew's icy blue eyes, these details returned vividly. A circle formed; a solid ring of young bodies each claiming a front-row position and, as a group, effectively locking out adult intervention. He had been aware of Blake egging him on. After the standoff, Andrew lay flat on the floor, bleeding. The scene ended with staff dispersing the crowd and summoning an ambulance.

"Devon!"

Snapping to high alert Devon saw his father and the principal standing before him. Judgment time.

"You and Blake are free to go," said the principal. "No point in returning to class, there's only 20 minutes left in the day. Be on time tomorrow." He shook Devon's father's hand and headed back to his inner sanctum.

The boys followed Devon's father to the parking lot in silence. There was no lecture about embarrassing the family, or immature behavior. Devon voiced his confusion.

"You're just lucky to have such a good friend," said his father. "That Westerlake girl explained it all. She said Hardwick verbally assaulted her. He sounds like a real jerk. Cassie said you stepped up to make him stop being abusive. She described how food spilled as students rushed to get out of the way. Then, when Andrew took a swing, which you ducked, he lost his balance. She made it clear Andrew fell, rather than being pushed."

Devon's father grinned as he navigated to Blake's neighbourhood. "I've gotta admit, Dev. When they called me I expected the worst. I gotta apologize, kiddo; I misjudged you. Cassie said you were calm. Described you as a gentleman. Ha! I guess you'll be a Facebook hero for a day. Cassie said the crowd applauded when Andrew hit the floor. Ha! I think maybe that girl has a crush on you, Dev."

Devon rolled down the window, leaned his face into the breeze and spit out his gum.

Marion Reidel

Call of Support

"Hello?"

"Hi Beth? It's Andy. How's my big sister?"

"Fine, Andrew, but I'm just on my way out. What's up?"

"Well... I just heard about Taylor, and... I thought I should call."

"Taylor? Oh, you mean her new job? She —"

"No. Mom told me Taylor has a... girlfriend."

"Yes..."

"Well, I just wanted to let you know, that... well... Cheryl and I still love her anyway."

"Love her anyway? What is that supposed to mean?"

"Despite her... you know... her choice. She's still family to us. We'll always be there for her, even though she's decided to be... you know... gay."

"Honest to God Andrew, I can't believe you're saying this. You love her *anyway*? Like she has some disease? Taylor hasn't *chosen* to be gay, Andrew. It's who she is. It's not a decision."

"Then how come at 18 years old she suddenly has a girlfriend?"

"There has been no sudden change, you are just totally unaware. Taylor has had a series of same sex relationships since high school. She has always been gay, Andrew. She was born that way."

"I just thought she was a tomboy."

"Well, you thought wrong."

"Listen, don't get mad at me, Beth. I called to be support-ive. This isn't easy for Cheryl and me, you know. Cheryl's very devout and Taylor's —"

"Taylor's what?"

"I don't know the right word. Alternative lifestyle?"

"Wrong on both counts, Andrew. Being gay is not a *life-style*. It is an intrinsic part of a person's nature. Like I said before, it is not a choice. It is who they are. And… the word *alternative* suggests that there is a right way of living and Taylor is living in some manner other than the right way. Can you hear how offensive that is?"

"I'm not talking about right and wrong, Beth. Shit! I know it's becoming acceptable. I read the papers. I've heard about gay marriages. I am not an idiot. It's just that Cheryl and I have no experience with this. You've gotten used to it, but we just found out. I am trying to offer my support. I'm sorry if I've used the wrong words. I have two normal kids so I don't know all the gay jargon like you do."

"Oh, my God! You are so offensive. I can't believe you just said that. I've really got to go."

"Wait a minute! I am your only brother and I am trying to connect here. Help me out a bit, will ya? I am not trying to upset you. I called to say I am okay with this. I don't know what I've done wrong."

"You've done just about *everything* wrong. Taylor is your niece. You've known her all her life and she is not someone different just because you have learned she has a girlfriend instead of a boyfriend."

"That's what I said. I still love her."

"Arrrgh! Still? That implies she's done something wrong,

you idiot. You just finished saying you don't understand the situation because you have two *normal* kids. Don't you see you're implying that Taylor is *abnormal?"*

"I don't mean abnormal as in unacceptable. I mean… different. You've got to admit, Beth, being a lesbian is different."

"And people who are *different* are persecuted."

"I am not persecuting her. I called to offer my support."

"You're missing the point, Andrew. If Mom had told you Taylor had a boyfriend, would you have called to say you love her anyway?"

"Well… probably not. But that's because —"

"That's because, whether you admit it to yourself or not, you made the judgment there is something wrong with Taylor having a girlfriend and so you are calling because you want to tell me you 'still love her' despite this abnormal aspect of Taylor's life. Right?"

"I don't know what you expect me to do, Beth."

"Nothing. I expect you to do nothing."

"What do you mean? You want me to disappear?"

"No, just don't make a fuss. Like I said, Taylor is the same person she always has been. Her partner Leanne is a fabulous person and they're good for each other. Taylor has a new job as administrative assistant for the Yorktown Youth Centre and Leanne is a dental hygienist. They have a great apartment in the city and are happy, responsible citizens. The reason Mom mentioned Leanne to you is because the girls went to visit her last weekend. Mom's been really lonely since Dad died and they took her out for lunch. When was the last time your kids visited their grandmother, Andrew?"

"Now you're not being fair, Beth. Taylor is older and has a car. My kids have no way of getting there."

"Right."

"Okay, here's what I think. I think you are being super defensive because you're worried about Taylor's lifestyle, or life choice, or whatever the hell the politically correct term is. Historically gays have been persecuted and you're afraid that, even though things are changing, Taylor will face prejudice, or even hatred."

"Exactly. Even from her family."

"That's where you've gone overboard. I am *not* expressing hatred. Maybe I chose the wrong words. I guess I have a lot to learn, but I called to say I love my niece and this is not going to change that. I thought you would welcome my call, not tear a strip off of me. Shit! I can learn the right language. Isn't the important part that I love my niece?"

"You said you love her despite who she is."

"I said I love her as I have always loved her."

"But you were unaware of how offensive your message sounds."

"I am now. I apologize and I will try to do better in the future. I need you to help me."

"I am tired of educating people on this issue. I shouldn't have to."

"But you do have to. Shit Beth, it hasn't been so long since gays were imprisoned, or forced into chemical castrations. It's only recently that high-profile gay people, like actors, designers, musicians, even athletes are coming out of the closet."

"That's right, Andrew, but it's *easier* for them to gain acceptance because they are rich and famous. It's your gay neighbour, shopkeeper, teacher or police officer who has the hardest time."

"That's because we don't *suspect* them."

"WHAT?"

"Calm down. It was a joke."

Marion Reidel

Mother-of-the-Bride

Celeste's Merlot spilled as she rose to address the bridal shower guests. "Can I have everyone's attention? Everyone? Excuse me! Listen up… please. Oh, don't fuss over that, Beth. A little soda water will take it out. It's not as if your carpet doesn't have other war wounds."

The cheerful chattering stopped abruptly as the guests observed Beth, their hostess, on hands and knees as if paying homage to the mother-of-the-bride. Brushing imaginary crumbs from her tailored turquoise suit, Celeste relaxed her shoulders, drew a deep breath and smoothed the side of her French bun in preparation for delivering her speech.

"As I look around, I see my nearest and dearest friends in all the world. I can't tell you how honoured I am that you, *my* friends, have gathered here in Beth's cozy, but not quite mortgage free, home to bring your best wishes to *my* daughter, Tiffany." Celeste beamed, as those gathered offered delicate applause, warm smiles, followed by gracious head nods and hand pats to the individuals seated adjacent.

"Some of you have daughters who are married, so you will understand my situation." Nodding was paired with murmurs of affirmation. Celeste injected a dramatic pause before continuing. "They say a wedding is all about the bride, and my Tiffany certainly subscribes to that school of thought. Don't you, sweetheart? But *we* know better, don't we girls?" More murmurs of agreement as Celeste admired the perfection of her professional manicure.

"Weddings are very challenging for mothers-of-the-bride. It is on our shoulders that the success of the day rests. I will admit to you, my good friends, over the last few weeks my nerves have been so frazzled that Charles has found every excuse to get out of the house and the cat won't curl up in my lap." Celeste's laugh, as light as fluttering wings, was echoed by her audience. "Charles spends most of his afternoons at the country club with the boys. He takes his golf clubs, but from the smell of his breath, I know he spends more time sipping bourbon in the bar than he does on the fairway. You know how it is? Right, ladies?" A further flutter of supportive giggles.

"I guess I shouldn't be surprised. Sandy, you remember how we met our men in that smelly campus bar? What was it called? O'Flannigan's? O'Hannigan's? O'Houlihan's? Something Irish anyway. We probably should've known that a university watering hole was not a suitable hunting ground for the fathers of our future children. But we did delight in shocking our parents. Didn't we?" Celeste paused to permit a short burst of reminiscent rumbling. "I guess I should be grateful. At least Charles has stuck around to maintain my lifestyle. Sandy, you had no way of knowing Robert would become a 'switch hitter,' as they say. We always thought his mannerisms were just part of his artistic nature. Remember?" Sandy appeared to receive a phone call and gestured an excuse to leave the room.

"Anyway, several of you have asked me about the details of the upcoming wedding ceremony. You probably expected it to be held at St. Jude's. Father Prescott asked if he should set aside a date for Tiffany. After all, St Jude's is where she was baptized and confirmed, but Tiff insists she is not having a formal church ceremony. Isn't that right, honey? I will admit I am at a bit of a loss to explain what Tiff's plan is. But you all know I'm not the type to interfere or press my opinions upon anyone, so I have stayed well out of the way as she made the arrangements. Haven't I, darling?" Tiffany whispered something to her bridesmaid.

"I guess I should be content with the fact that she is getting married at all." Celeste paused just long enough to invite supportive laughter. She cast a rehearsed world-weary smile in all directions. "Yes, I should be grateful indeed, because I can still remember how *your* heart was broken, Janice, when Angela got pregnant and ran off with that hoodlum. How many years has it been since she's spoken to you? Three? Gosh, I'd just perish if I even had to go three days without talking to my beloved Tiffany. Wouldn't I, Pumpkin? I know it had been a very trying time for you, Janice, and I would have liked to have been there to support you, but you'll recall Charles and I had already booked our getaway to Punta Marta and those tickets were absolutely non-refundable. It was just impossible timing." Celeste placed her hand lightly on her chest.

"It's because you managed to handle the trauma of Angela's betrayal, Janice, and Sandy dealt with Amber's weight problem so well, and you, Beth, are absolutely a rock about Taylor's gender confusion... I know you *all* understand the stress I've been under." Celeste paused to acknowledge Janice who pointed towards the washroom, and Karen indicating she would accompany Janice.

"Now Tiff, I don't mean this as a criticism. I'm just bonding with my friends. Ladies, I'm sure you will empathize when I tell you… I have *not* been consulted on any of the wedding plans. I have not seen a menu, nor the floral centrepiece design, nor the music selection, not even the tablecloth colours. Why, I didn't see an invitation until mine arrived in the mail. It's shocking, I know. In my own way I feel just as abandoned as Janice did when Angela eloped." The group's muttered response escalated.

"Ladies, you will also understand the stress I am suffering when I tell you about the groom's family… Where are you going, Tiff? A smoke? That's not very ladylike, Cupcake. It won't do on your wedding day. Brittany, as maid of honour you should be helping her give up that filthy habit. Hurry back, girls. Now, what was I saying? Oh yes, the groom's family. I don't know how I'm expected to have rapport with these strangers and share my grandchildren. Don't misunderstand me, they are lovely people. We were invited for dinner two weeks ago. Their little house is very tidy. I can certainly understand why Tiff's fiancé has never moved out. My goodness, why would he leave when his mother is providing his meals and doing his laundry?" This insight was met by laughter, but Celeste noticed the hostess, Beth, had retreated to the kitchen and poured straight vodka into a coffee mug.

Her audience's attention enveloped her like the softest of pashminas, so Celeste confidently continued. "His relationship with his parents is not at all like the one Charles and I have with Geoffrey. When Geoffrey went off to university, we made it very clear he was not expected to return home. His old bedroom serves me beautifully as a scrap-booking studio, in which my creativity has blossomed. Of course you all know this, being the recipients of my bedazzled greeting cards. Charles and I have helped Geoffrey grow as an individual by pushing him down the path to adulthood, and Geoffrey is proud of his little bachelor flat. You'd never know it's in a basement because his special "grow lights" create a very bright atmosphere, which has been good for Geoffrey's depression. And his landlord, a lovely foreign fellow, responded promptly to deal with the infestation. Geoffrey has said several times how glad he is not to be living at home anymore."

"But I digress... I was telling you about Tiff's future in-laws. They are lovely, and they have done very well for themselves in Canada. I am impressed that people can succeed without mastering the English language. They can do everything; shopping, doctors, church and socializing in their native tongue. Who knew? It is equally impressive their offspring speak English without a trace of an accent. I guess that proves how excellent our public school system is. You'd never know they were immigrants at all." Celeste reached for her refilled drink, savouring the power of commanding an audience. She wondered if she should run for the presidency of the *Always Helping Others League*.

"And the meal... now that was something else. The woman makes *everything* from scratch. The vegetables were from her garden, there was homemade bread, even the wine was made in the basement. Gosh, all we have in *our* basement is a home theatre. Oh, and there are *two* kitchens in the house. The one beside the dining room seemed to be a show kitchen, but the real work happened in the garage. I think it is something about keeping the smell of fish and cabbage out of the house." Again Celeste felt encouraged to see the shower guests sharing reactions amongst themselves. One guest rose to gather empty plates and indicated her intention to check on Beth in the kitchen.

"You all know I eat like a bird. It's a necessity to keep my youthful figure," Celeste said as she smoothed invisible creases from her suit, "so I found it challenging to endure the five-course meal. I felt it was essential to take a taste of everything so as not to offend." Celeste turned to address the woman perched on the arm of a chair to her right. "Wendy, I employed your old trick of breaking up the food and moving it around on the plate to make it appear as if I had eaten. I often thank God for giving me an anorexic roommate because you taught me so many practical skills at university." Celeste could sense the warmth of the group's admiration as she turned to glance out the front window to check on Tiffany and Brittany. They were smoking and laughing as they leaned against Tiff's red Miata.

"So, we survived the meeting with the in-laws," she continued as she glared at the girls, trying to mentally command them to return to the party. "I took them a bottle of French red so they could taste what *real* wine is like. They set it aside to drink by themselves and I'm sure they'll enjoy it. I also brought along Tiffany's baby album, but Tiff would not let me take it out of my bag. She wasn't able to explain in front of them, but I suspect she felt they might be intimidated by what a fabulous childhood she had. No need to emphasize the disparity in family backgrounds." Tiffany and Brittany got into Tiff's car. *Ungrateful bitches!*

"Oh, you know what else I've had to deal with? I can be totally candid now that Tiff has stepped out," Celeste said as she watched Tiffany's car pull away from the curb. She continued to face the window so her friends would not read the tension in her clenched jawline. "There are no bridesmaids, other than Brittany, so I have no clear colour scheme on which to base my dress. Oh yes, I know, you are shocked that I still have not purchased my mother-of-the-bride outfit. And... as you saw on the invitation, the ceremony is going to be held in a tent on a farm owned by a friend of the groom. Why, I don't know whether I should wear high heels or gum boots. It's outrageous. And what if it rains? Being expected to cope with mud is more than I can bear."

As Tiff's car disappeared around the corner at the end of the block, Celeste felt time stand still. She couldn't move or even breathe. Her thoughts switched to slow motion. She had pleaded to get her daughter to attend this event. She needed to put a positive spin on Tiff's departure. Celeste understood her friends were the only people she could depend on. Tilting her chin up to elongate her aging neck Celeste angled her face so the light from the window illuminated her skin beautifully. She kept her back to the room, knowing the lines of her tailored suit hung perfectly. She confided in them. "The only thought sustaining me in this time of great stress is the possibility of having all of you, *my dearest friends*, in that mucky tent with me."

"I want to let you ladies know how much I appreciate your support," Celeste said, feeling her pulse settle back to a regular rhythm. "After all, these young people don't have friends who can afford to buy them decent wedding gifts. It's up to us to get the newlyweds the crystal and china that makes a real home. Am I right?" At the lack of response

Celeste turned to discover a nearly empty room. Her second cousin, Polly, slumped on the couch, mouth agape and drool running down her chin, and Beth's elderly neighbour, Mrs. Ecclestone, was devouring the last of the canapés.

Celeste sipped her wine and returned to looking out the window. She comforted herself with words from her favourite motivational speaker, Pastor John Maxwell, *"When the pressure is on, great leaders are at their best. Whatever is inside them comes to the surface."* She understood this to be a test.

Wedding Toast

Thunder rumbled in the distance as the wedding guests meandered towards the shelter of the Parties R Us tent. Net drapery and twinkle lights rustled as the wind followed the attendees through the archways. From his hideaway behind the tent, the Best Man studied the clouds. He had stepped into the shadows so he could have a smoke and steady his nerves. Repeated attempts to ignite his lighter failed, so he finally threw his virgin cigarette to the ground and crushed it under the heel of his shoe. Absentmindedly, he slipped the nonfunctional lighter back into his pocket and headed toward the tent's entrance.

Freely flowing alcohol had washed over the wedding guests since mid-afternoon, causing chatter and boisterous laughter to roll through the confined space. Another remote rumble, like a transport truck approaching over an iron bridge, was echoed by static crackling over the PA system. The Best Man held the microphone at arm's length, between two fingers, like a poisonous snake.

"Hello? Hello? Can you hear me?" Despite his anxious attempts, the Best Man found it difficult to disengage the guests from their merriment to focus them on the formalities. He tapped his spoon against the rim of his wineglass, inadvertently expanding a previously imperceptible crack, just as the bride's great-uncle misjudged the location of his chair and landed on his backside with a bleated curse. Once again the group's attention was drawn away from the head table as the inebriated uncle was helped to his feet.

"Hello? Testing. Can you hear me now?" The Best Man looked to his right and saw the groom toss back another scotch. Setting down his drained tumbler Theo gave a thumbs-up signal, then in one smooth gesture, checked his watch, swept an errant hair from his forehead and draped his arm over the back of his bride's chair. Theo cast a condescending smile in his bride's direction, then repositioned a bread knife so he could check his reflection.

As people struggled in the confined space, trying to locate their seats, the buzz of conversation began to subside. Glasses were refilled, then serving staff withdrew. The guests' bleary gazes turned to the head table. "Hello? Hello? Can you hear me now?" The Best Man shrugged, set down the faulty microphone, and sank to his chair. As he contemplated the situation, he wondered how the hell he got himself into this mess. He had known Theo since preschool. The new Canadian neighbours needed support and the Best Man's mother had been only too happy to oblige. Throughout their childhood Theo became a constant presence in the Best Man's home. Their relationship evolved into a constant need to outdo each other. He considered Theo an opponent more than *friend*.

A flash and rumble caused the Best Man to flinch. He remembered a childhood adventure. A summer spent at Scout camp where he shared a cabin with Theo and four other boys. There was a violent thunderstorm on the second-last night of their stay. Theo, in an attempt to impress the others, or just amuse himself, had locked his *best friend* outside in the storm. The Best Man recalled huddling beneath a huge pine in an attempt to find shelter from the wind and rain, yet terrified that a lightning strike could destroy him.

The Best Man's nerves grew more frazzled as he watched a staff member attempt to fix the malfunctioning sound system. The serving crew reappeared to deliver another round of drinks, and the guests resumed their animated conversations. Boisterous laughter transformed into shrieks accented by the clatter of glassware. The guests were milling about again; the Best Man toyed with the idea of bolting.

Scanning the crowd, the Best Man heard the patter of rain on the plastic tent increase. Additional catering staff arrived armed with rolls of arched plastic windows to secure the tent from moisture. The drumming of the rain triggered another memory of how his competition with Theo began. On a rainy afternoon, four year-old Theo proclaimed a schoolyard challenge to see who could eat the biggest worm. The Best Man had been so desperate to be accepted by the gregarious dark-haired Theo that he would have eaten a boa constrictor.

As the years passed, their competition progressed to include academic achievement, athletic awards and accumulating the symbols of success. When he was seventeen years old Theo's uncle gave him a perfectly refurbished vintage red Mustang with a white ragtop and V8 engine, while the Best Man inherited a rusting grey Volvo sedan when his grandmother could no longer drive. Theo dated a series of cheerleaders, and served as starting point guard on his varsity basketball team, while the Best Man played trumpet in the band that roused the fans. Theo had infiltrated his life more than a brother could... and he hated Theo.

"Welcome everyone. Welcome." The damn technicians had fixed the sound system; the show must go on. "As best man it is my honour to say…" A brilliant flash drove any further thought from his mind. A clap of thunder vibrated the tent, causing startled shrieks and nervous giggles to erupt from the crowd. The pace of the rain mimicked a snare drum and the wind beat against the plastic walls with desperation. *Say what?* Suddenly he felt panic. *What was he meant to say? Where were his notes?* Theo had co-written the perfect toast to the groom, a long list of compliments, a shameless tribute to Theo's masculine perfection, a list of lies.

The Best Man caught the bride's eye as Theo assured her that the storm posed no threat. Tiffany appeared to be a classic beauty, but desperation for Theo's approval overpowered her self-esteem. She had been snared like a butterfly in a web and there was no way to release her now without causing more harm.

The Best Man located his notes. Nowhere in the groom's approved text did it mention the time he provided an alibi when Theo cheated on his fiancée, now his wife of a few hours. It didn't mention the money Theo borrowed over the years, yet never paid back. No comment about the second year essay Theo plagiarized, the time he totaled his parents' car when driving drunk, the girl he got pregnant that summer on the coast, or how his new father-in-law handed Theo a top level corporate job he was not qualified for.

Another flash and immediate bang caused the wedding guests to clutch their neighbours. A short series of instantaneous lightning and thunder bursts felt like the storm was fighting to come inside the tent. The rain had been beating down on the temporary reception hall when, without warning, an accumulation of water which had caused an inconspicuous bulge in the graceful curve of the tent's canopy suddenly split the plastic and cascaded on a cluster of aunties, each dressed in a different pastel shade of synthetic chiffon. They screeched as icy rainwater rushed down the back of their dresses.

Once again the Best Man paused the proceedings while waiters and ushers hurried to mop up the drenched aunties. He used the time to mentally rehearse his comments and found it impossible to focus on the sanctioned script as he obsessed about Theo's constant demand for loyalty. He had lied for Theo and had taken the blame for Theo's mistakes and misdeeds. The image of Theo's perfectly symmetrical features was burned into the Best Man's memory along with the sordid details of how Theo cheated on Tiffany during their engagement. He wondered whether, as Best Man, he was obligated to warn Tiff that she faced a future of marital deceit. Should he warn the father-in-law of Theo's adept dishonesty and polished procrastination? He had never hated anyone more than Theo. While savouring the satisfaction of mentally exorcising his pent-up anger, an usher gestured from the back of the tent that the sodden aunties were settled and the toast to the groom could resume.

The Best Man glanced at the groom who gave him another enthusiastic nod and thumbs-up signal. The bride smiled with fragile composure, her back stiff, hands neatly clasped on the table's edge, and facial muscles clenched in an expression of hopeful optimism. Twinkle lights hung above her hair, creating the impression of a halo and casting a flattering glow over her features. He asked himself, *Does she know what she's done? Perhaps I should address my comments to*

Tiffany. I could tell her Theo is a fraud, liar and cheat. She's been taken in by misleading packaging. Her life with Theo will be a series of putdowns and disappointments.

The rain seemed to be letting up as the thunder rumbled in the distance, moving on to disrupt other lives. Stillness overtook the tent as the guests settled in their seats. Glasses had been topped-up and once again the serving staff withdrew. People seemed more anesthetized than attentive. The blood alcohol level of the guests rendered them inert. They no longer had the energy to be raucous, and their glassy eyes were unable to focus as the Best Man rose once more.

A total hush settled and all eyes were trained on the head table as the Best Man grasped the microphone, then shifted it to his other hand. He took a deep breath, silently asked for God's guidance and began, "Ladies and gentlemen… actually, what I have to say should be addressed to you, Tiffany."

"They call me 'The Best Man,' but we all know that no one measures up to your groom. The gods blessed him with the beauty of Adonis, and wisdom beyond his years. He has earned more gold medals and trophies than most Olympic competitors, and he graduated in the top five percent of his class. Now Theo has found his perfect partner in you, beautiful Tiffany, and together you are ready to embark on a storybook life. Theo scored a prestigious position as a junior partner in your family's firm. There will be plenty of expense account lunches and golf course meetings for him. Thanks to your father's generosity, you have a suburban palace waiting for you to fill it with babies. And they will be damn good-looking ones."

He raised his glass and said, "Ladies and gentlemen, I ask you to rise and lift your glasses in a toast to Theo and Tiffany."

At that moment a ferocious gust of wind rattled the tent, yanking several lines from their anchor pegs. Guests were roused from their lethargic state and china rattled as people clutched their tables in an automatic response to anchor themselves. Through the plastic archways the illumination of the grounds could be seen as lightning struck a tree 100 metres from the tent. It toppled to the ground with a crunching sound. There was a surge in the electrical system, and behind the head table, the Best Man collapsed.

Marion Reidel

The Fireman

It had been a combustible orgasm. As he inhaled deeply, the aroma of incineration teased Blake's nostrils. He could taste the charred deliciousness of the fire's remains. Kicking the sodden debris with his steel-toed boot, Blake checked for hot spots, hidden embers, which might reignite.

He'd been safely in bed when the call came at 3:00 a.m. The cottage property, on Pine Cliff Trail, had been closed up all winter. Blake had no sympathy for arrogant city people who invaded his community each summer. They'd be delighted to rebuild, something bigger, more stylish. This had been one of the lake's original cottages. Nice dry timber, lots of lovely books, with a little improperly stored gasoline in the shed.

The location was ten minutes from Blake's house, but he preferred not to arrive first. He monitored his CB radio and rolled up right after the chief. By then the tiny cottage had become fully ablaze. Flames spit thirty feet into the air, creating a wave of heat that kept the volunteers well back. They could only wet the surrounding pines. The potential for a forest fire aroused him.

Blake continued stirring the rubble and adding water. After five hours on the scene he still felt a buzz of erotic energy. His clothes would smell of smoke for days. He could relive the gratification for weeks.

A glint of metal reflected the weak morning light. Blake crouched to extricate a locket, made of silver with a long chain. He looked over his shoulder before slipping the keepsake into his pocket. He stood, stretching his back, and wiped the sweat off his forehead. Blake smiled.

He'd been content with the satisfaction that property destruction provided, but recently, he discovered the bonus of valuables among the aftermath. In his modest home at the Sunshine Acres Trailer Park, he had transformed the broom closet into a gallery for his treasures. It was often jewelry he made off with, but there'd also been a coin collection, heirloom silver, and war medals. Blake collected bits of shiny metal like a magpie.

Anonymity empowered his recreational arson. His appearance was nondescript; just another medium height clean-shaven white guy with brown hair and no glasses. He dressed in clothing from the local farm supply store, generic navy chinos and matching shirts. He wore a ball cap like everyone else in town, no logo, brim pointed forward. Nothing about Blake drew attention.

His hobby began around puberty. His life had been good up until his tenth birthday. He lived in a bungalow on Charles Street right across from the town's park. He had been the only child of Tony and Jen Brooks. Their little trio spent hours in the park, on the swing, in the sandbox, having picnics, surrounded by a bubble of love so intense it cast a glow.

As Blake got older, the park visits involved soccer matches and pickup softball. He inherited athletic ability. Tony had been a high school track star; Jen danced. They'd fallen in love during their senior year and had married soon after graduation, because Blake was on the way. Tony got a job at the mill, Jen stayed home with the baby, and later took in other kids for a fee. It felt like paradise.

During that tenth summer the unimaginable happened. Blake's mother killed his father. It hadn't been intentional, but she did it all the same. They'd left Blake at home with the fourteen-year-old from next door; Cindy with the braces and thick glasses. Tony and Jen had gone to a friend's wedding. A couple they knew from high school. The pair had gone on to college; started careers before getting married. The wedding took place in town to accommodate their families, but they had no intention of returning to "Hicksville." They were destined for better things.

The fatal argument started at the reception. Tony and Jen had too much to drink. She expressed jealousy of the newly-weds, felt trapped. He blamed her for getting pregnant. Could have made something of himself, instead of getting stuck in a dead-end job. The conflict escalated. Jen wouldn't let Tony drive home. She wrestled the keys from him, causing Tony to fall and bang his head on the car's fender. She laughed at her collapsed husband, mocked his masculinity. He threw-up, then dragged himself into the car's backseat.

Jen continued ranting. Tony, blissfully unaware of her scathing remarks and totally relaxed, was crushed to death when Jen ran a red light. She told the story to the police in excruciating detail when they arrested her. A transport truck t-boned the Brooks' sedan nearly severing the rear portion of the vehicle. The jaws-of-life freed Jen. Tony was compacted. Jen received four years for involuntary manslaughter, for her role in Tony's death sentence.

* * *

Blake spent the morning after the cottage fire in the coffee shop. He fiddled with his lukewarm coffee while caressing the locket hidden in his pants. He liked the smooth hard surface, and how he could feel the intricate etched design. It reminded him of the locket his mother wore, containing images of her two *men*.

He watched Bea, the waitress, as she served customers with warm enthusiasm. An old lady approached the counter to place her order. She reminded Blake of his Nana. She had the same blue hair and bent back. Nana had looked after Blake, not only while Jen served her time in prison, but also after she was released. No one trusted Jen to babysit anymore, so she took up full-time drinking. For all Blake knew that's what she was still doing. On interview nights, teachers told Nana that Blake's behavior was withdrawn and socially awkward. He found it difficult to make friends. Blake assured Nana there was no one at school worth being friends with. Nana's now gone. She'd lived long enough to see Blake graduate from high school, but then the cancer got her. At least she'd left a trust fund and bungalow to Jen so Blake didn't have to look after his mother.

To say Blake felt angry about the loss of his father would be like saying a tornado is windy. His insides sometimes felt like an overwound clock spring, vibrating with tension, waiting to be released, until he discovered his passion for flames. It had been a happy accident. While Blake walked home from high school, a sudden thunderstorm struck. He'd taken cover in the hardware store's doorway and witnessed lightning torch the park's largest tree. The suddenness combined with the reverberating thunderclap made every cell in Blake's body tingle. The phallic imagery of the ignited pine went beyond Blake's understanding at the time, but his body responded. It felt… satisfying.

Page 100

High school had been hell for Blake. He and his only friend, Devon, were social outcasts. Their depression illustrated by the black hoodies for which they became known. It was then his invisibility began.

After months of frustration, Blake found the courage to recreate the experience. He tried wandering during storms and following fire trucks, with no success. To take control, he devised a plan. He began small. A match tossed into the washroom garbage can resulted in a favourable school evacuation and the arrival of the town's fire trucks, but no flames to enjoy. He moved on to the Dumpster behind the Fresh Fields grocery store, but the boxes were damp and hard to ignite. A little shoplifting at the hardware store offered the solution in the form of lighter fluid. Well named, he realized.

Blake developed a formula for gratification. Identify something combustible, that could be contained, with no threat to human life, (Blake was not a killer... not like his mother) then, add an accelerant. This had to be managed carefully. He found it best to use something near at hand, so it seemed spontaneous. Since the Dumpster incident at fifteen, Blake had burned three sheds, a boathouse, a camper van in storage, the town dump multiple times, and now his second cottage.

His compulsion intensified in both frequency and magnitude. The next challenge to overcome was explaining his presence at these events. When he turned nineteen, he joined the volunteer fire department. Once again, life seemed good.

Blake took his empty mug up to the counter where Bea wiped the surface. She was a platinum-haired beauty with a body straining to escape from her polyester uniform. One of these days those buttons would pop and Blake prayed he would be present to witness it.

"Thanks, Blake," Bea chirped as she accepted the mug. "I'm so dog tired I was avoiding the hike to your table."

She had referred to him by name. She saw him. Blake went speechless.

"I hear you boys had a big one out on Pine Cliff Trail last night. Bobby said the place went up like kindling. Wish I coulda seen it," she said.

"You like fires?"

"Well, nobody *likes* fires, but it musta been awesome. Bobby said the flames were twenty feet tall and the heat was blisterin'."

"Thirty."

"What?"

"Thirty. The flames were thirty feet tall," Blake corrected. "Pretty near set the whole forest ablaze." He fondled the locket in his pocket and dropped his gaze to the floor. "Hot as a furnace," he mumbled, but Bea had already moved down the counter to serve another customer. The connection broke.

That night Blake lay in bed fantasizing. Bea was significantly older than him, divorced with a kid, but that didn't concern him. Mothers often abandoned their children. He could tell Bea felt attracted to him. She had called him by name. Said she would have liked to see the fire. He would make a fire for her... a spectacular fire located so she couldn't miss it, but not too soon. He began eating at the diner every second day as he developed a plan.

* * *

Two weeks before executing his plan, Blake brought Bea a couple of coins from his collection. They were embossed with characters from Greek mythology. He said he found them in the roadside gravel near the trailer park. "I thought your kid might enjoy them. He could pretend it's pirate treasure, or look them up on the computer and see where they're from."

"Well, aren't you just the sweetest thing?" said Bea. "You sure you wanna give 'em away? Might be worth something."

"I doubt it," said Blake. "If they were valuable, they wouldn't have been tossed on the road." Blake briefly wondered if he should step in and show the kid what a father should be like. Bea refilled his coffee and slipped the coins in the tiny pocket on the left breast of her peach uniform.

Blake had a simple plan. Bea's kid would be at school, so her house would be empty, not even a pet to worry about. She lived a block from the diner in a small clapboard cottage nearly hidden by shrubbery. The overgrowth made it easy to approach without being seen. He'd discovered that Bea was a hoarder. Her back veranda had piles of boxes, newspapers and bags of old clothes. At the side of the house he found an abandoned gas lawn mower. Blake didn't know if it contained any fuel, but it didn't matter. Its proximity meant the investigators would make the desired assumptions. Once Bea was rendered homeless, Blake would offer to share his home.

* * *

While Blake prepared a small can of oil and gasoline mix, suitable for a mower, an unanticipated complication arrived at the diner.

Bea poured coffee for Constable Brown as he laid the two coins on the counter. "So, did you find out about 'em? I'm dead curious," said Bea.

"I can tell you exactly where they came from," the constable replied. He set his hat on the counter, noticed the buttons straining over Bea's bosom, added three sugars to his coffee and loosened his belt by one notch. "These coins are on an inventory at the County Office. You remember a couple years back, the big cottage that burned down on the north side of the lake?"

"Yeah. Some folks from Toronto owned it. Still haven't rebuilt. Right?"

"Yeah. They submitted a list of everything destroyed in the fire. It included a coin collection. The guy was very specific."

"And these coins are on the list?"

"You betcha. Apparently they're valuable."

* * *

Blake crept along the side of the house. A dog barked in the next yard and he froze, heart pounding, but the neighbour yelled *shut up* and it did. He continued his stealthy progress and poured the fuel on the porch debris, taking care not to spill any on himself.

* * *

Bea offered Constable Brown a piece of apple pie to go with his coffee. "This is surely a mystery," she said. "A valuable foreign coin from all the way t'other side of the lake. Do ya think an animal mighta carried it here?"

"I doubt it."

"You know, crows like shiny things."

"These don't look very shiny," said Brown.

"They've bin lying on the road for two years."

"More likely someone scavenged the fire site. You said they were found at Sunny Acres, could be someone from the trailer park."

"Yeah… Hey, 'cuse me. I'm gonna call Tommy. He's home from school today with the flu. This mystery'll cheer him up." Bea looked around to ensure all the patrons' needs were met before picking up the phone beside the cash register.

* * *

Blake ignited the debris with a lighter. Best not to risk leaving a match. The boxes went *whoosh* and the back porch was ablaze. Blake withdrew to the alley, unseen, and circled the block. He'd appear once the neighbours were on the street. Easy to sidle up when you're invisible.

* * *

Bea's call woke her son. He'd been asleep on the couch with the TV playing cartoons. As he spoke to his mother he headed to the bathroom carrying the cordless receiver. At the rear of the house he stopped, unable to process what he saw.

"Maw, the back porch is lit up."

"Sorry, honey. I must have left the light on this morning. Just flip the switch by the back door."

"No, Maw. It's… it's on fire. All I can see out the window is fire." The rear window suddenly burst inward. Tommy was struck in the temple by a piece of the frame and crumpled to the floor, dropping the phone.

"Tommy! Tommy!" Bea also dropped her receiver. She turned towards Constable Brown in what seemed like slow motion. "I think my house is on fire and Tommy's inside."

Bea felt teleported to her front lawn. One moment she stood behind the counter at the diner, talking to Tommy on the phone, the next she was on the lawn watching her house burn. Shock blinded her to Constable Brown's efficiency. He'd scooped her into his patrol car while talking to the dispatcher. The fire truck arrived and volunteers scrambled to get organized.

Blake stepped up beside Bea. He didn't like the way the cop had his arm around her shoulder. She stood absolutely still, hands busy twisting her apron, tears streaming down her cheeks, saying nothing. Blake had expected her to be upset about losing her possessions, he would make it up to her.

"Don't worry Bea. They're just things. It can all be replaced," said Blake.

"You don't understand," she sobbed. "It's Tommy. He's in the house. I called him from the cafe and he said the house was on fire. "

Impossible. It was a school day. Blake saw the volunteers struggling to get the hoses off the truck and attached to the hydrant down the street. How could the kid be inside? Blake sprinted to the front door and rammed it with his shoulder. The frame gave way easily and he was only mildly aware of the shouts from the street telling him not to enter.

Inside the house Blake saw curtains burning and the ceiling falling. Through the smoke he spotted the kid curled on the floor with his arms protecting his head. Blake dodged a chunk of flaming ceiling and yanked the boy to his feet. He turned the boy to face the open doorway and yelled into his ear. "Don't worry about the flames. Get out the door. Your mother is waiting for you." He pushed the kid in the direction of the opening and watched him escape. Out the front window Blake could see the kid make it into his mother's arms and the volunteers approaching the house with hoses.

Blake scanned the smoke-filled room. A crocheted blanket, very much like the one his Nana made for him, draped over the couch where the boy had been sleeping. Cartoon animals frolicked on the TV with a surreal backdrop of burning curtains. Blake smiled. He closed his eyes, slid his hands into his pockets and caressed the locket. Something in the basement exploded and the floor gave way. Blake's last thought was, "Dad?"

* * *

A plaque in the town square commemorates Blake Brooks' heroic action. When the manager of the trailer park emptied Blake's unit, he discovered the closet full of treasures. Instead of reporting it, he took them to a Toronto pawnshop and kept the cash. Blake's tragic death began a fire-free period that lasted almost a decade. It wouldn't be until the summer Tommy Crawford turned seventeen when the cottagers would become careless again, setting their properties ablaze.

Marion Reidel

Breaking Through

Beth chewed the end of her paintbrush as she stared at a blank canvas. It was a Zen activity, meditative, and she'd been at it for two days. Her mind buzzed with white noise, like a television with no cable signal. She spat out a paint chip and set the brush down next to her palette with a sigh.

It had been three dreary days since Beth arrived at her family's cottage. She'd taken her vacation in May knowing that the place would be empty of family members, and the neighbours would also be absent. Beth spent the first day doing the season opening chores. She freshened bed linens, swept floors, set out the patio furniture, anything to avoid her true task.

She craved isolation, away from domestic demands and work commitments, to indulge the inner artist child who seemed to be playing hide-and-seek.

The picture window behind Beth's left shoulder shed midday light on the barren canvas. The illumination intensified the vast emptiness of the surface until it seemed to shriek in defiance. As she tucked stray hairs behind her right ear and began fidgeting with her earring, she wondered what her life might have been if she'd taken a different path. She decided to paint a landscape.

Beth reached for the tube of Chromium Oxide Green and squeezed a dollop on her palette next to the Ultramarine she already set out. She dipped a brush into fresh water and diluted the paint, then roughed in a horizon, shoreline and stand of evergreens. She'd made a start... it should be easy from here, she told herself. She confidently mapped out cloud formations and water texture with a wash of blue.

The smell of the paint took her back to college. She smiled as she pictured her twenty year-old self, confident, energetic, bursting with creativity. She used to spend hours debating poetry, music and art theory. Abstract concepts were treasures to be polished, displayed and exchanged. Paint encrusted the cuticles of her gnawed nails and her hair hung in braids embellished with feathers and beads. She escaped her small-town upbringing to the vibrancy of Toronto's core.

Something felt wrong. The trees were disproportionate, the composition off balance, the blue too intense. Her stomach rumbled. Beth wandered across the room and made a cup of blueberry tea. She put two shortbread cookies on a plate and brought the snack back to her painting table. She assessed the canvas and understood it was completely wrong.

After a tentative sip of steaming tea, Beth shoved a whole cookie in her mouth and grabbed a two-inch brush. She slopped water on her palette and mashed the blue and green pigments together. She slathered the aqua mixture across the surface, obliterating the offensive tree line. The result was a streaky blue texture that gave the impression of being under water. It felt like drowning.

She wondered what made her think she could paint. Sure, she'd been successful during college... years ago. She had been a completely different person then, afraid of nothing, eager to take risks, confident that she was adored. Her mind had overflowed with ideas and images. Being a mother drained her creative instincts. Daily decisions involved practical matters such as dinner menus and bank balances, rather than aesthetic ones, not to mention being abandoned. The shame of Randall's departure still clung to her. It would have been easier if he had died, got hit by a bus, succumbed to cancer, blew his brains out in the garage, but he'd just disappeared. Walked out of his life without a word.

Beth squeezed the bridge of her nose, then raked her fingers through her short mahogany hair, causing her to straighten her spine and sit taller. Using both hands she rubbed the back of her neck as she stretched and evaluated the banal blue painting. The colour was wrong. She didn't want blue. Blue seemed despondent; she sought energy. With renewed enthusiasm Beth squeezed Cadmium Red, Bright Orange, and Primary Yellow on a clean palette. Fire colours. The colours of passion and life. She picked up a brush, then set it aside in favour of a knife. Beth scraped up a slug of vibrant red-orange and applied a smooth layer over the suffocating water. She iced the canvas like a birthday cake. Precise and even, smoothing over any ridges or seams. Tension gathered in her shoulders as she gently stroked the surface, creating a silken sheen.

Tossing the palette knife on the table, she stood so abruptly her chair toppled and the easel threatened to collapse. Beth grabbed the second cookie and shoved it into her mouth, then began pacing the room. Randall's judgmental voice hijacked Beth's mind, driving away what little self-confidence she had mustered. Taking long, deliberate breaths, Beth struggled to banish her demon. Standing at the window she leaned her forehead against the glass and closed her eyes.

Tears slipped down Beth's cheek. She returned to pacing and gestured as she said aloud, "Who do you think you are?

Any idiot can buy art supplies, but you need to have talent to create art. Something you are sadly lacking, my friend. You had a chance, and you wasted it. Just like you've screwed up everything. Shitty wife… hopeless homemaker… no talent wannabe… Who do you think you are?"

On her seventh circuit Beth noticed the stereo and froze. A smile crept across her face as she reached into the CD collection and grabbed one of Taylor's favourites. She had to give herself permission to be a beginner, so… she would take a new approach. The tray of the player slid open and she inserted *Master of Puppets*. Beth pressed play and turned up the volume as Metallica assaulted the room. Taylor. Her precious angel had come into this world soft and pink, then, like a conjuring act turned into a leather-clad dynamo who'd been Beth's cheerleader. As the music pounded she could feel Taylor's strong embrace and musky scent. The one constant positive in Beth's life had been the support of her only child. It was Taylor who encouraged Beth to embark on this retreat.

Beth righted the chair and dragged it aside. She let the music direct her hand as she applied thick chunks of paint to the canvas in bold, slashing strokes. Holding the palette knife like a weapon, Beth attacked the surface, now standing, almost dancing, as she worked. She applied paint directly from the tube to the canvas then spread it blending the vibrant colours together. After an hour of frantic effort, Beth had smears of red pigment on her face and in her hair. She stood back to evaluate her work and… it was fabulous.

That evening, Beth made herself linguini with rich Alfredo sauce and poured a glass of chilled Pino Grigio. She lounged on the couch and admired the canvas displayed on her easel, backlit by the setting sun. Her senses worked in overdrive. She became aware of nuances in the music, now switched to Diana Krall, which previously eluded her. The taste and texture of the wine intrigued her and the commingling colours on the canvas seemed to be laughing with delight. Her body felt like she'd completed a workout, finished a great novel and fallen in love.

Marion Reidel

A Short Drive

Sandy's misery ended when she decided to drive her car into a bridge abutment. It was an old car, totally unreliable, a resale value of a few hundred dollars. No big loss.

Standing in her kitchen that afternoon, she brushed stray hairs off of her forehead as she reached for a spatula. Her hair used to be a lush, glossy black, but now coarse grey strands infiltrated, creating a wiry salt-and-pepper effect. Disturbingly like her mother's. Sandy gently stirred her grandma's pasta sauce recipe as she ruminated. She'd made it from scratch. She had stewed and skinned the tomatoes, added fresh oregano from her back porch and the Pinot Noir she'd made at the Wine Barn. Exactly as her mother had taught her. She extended her bottom lip and blew a burst of air to dislodge another stray strand that felt pasted to her forehead.

As she stirred the sauce, Sandy could hear her mother's voice as clearly as if she was present. "You're doing that wrong. You're always in such a hurry. Stir slowly. Draw the contents up from the bottom. Turn down the heat. Add more oregano. Your cheap wine is going to ruin it. You might as well have bought sauce in a jar."

Sandy's schedule included taking her mother to the heart specialist later in the week. It was always an ordeal to pick Mother up at the retirement home, bundle her and her walker into the car and endure the constant complaints. They would have to drive under the Hamilton Street Bridge to get to the Southtown Medical Centre. She pictured the wide cement facade on the bridge's right side. Sandy wiped her forehead with the back of her hand. She could never do it with Mother in the car.

Sandy sampled the sauce. It tasted bland. She added more wine and a dash of garlic salt. As she set the spice jar back in its rack the photos on her fridge caught her attention. She removed a ladybug magnet to free a snapshot taken at Camp Waseosa, the summer Amber had been ten and Devon eight. The image captured the trust on their faces, frozen in time, five years before their family would collapse.

Sandy stood at the kitchen counter, placed both hands at the base of her spine and stretched. She noticed the fingers of her right hand ached and were swollen as arthritis had crept in and defiled her joints. Eventually her hands would be crippled, like her mother's. She placed her palm on the cool granite and noticed her nails. Before Robert left she'd always had a professional manicure; nails painted some shade of glossy red, like *Big Apple* or *Manhattan Beach*. They used to make a satisfying click as she typed. Now her fingers had blunt ends. She'd revived her college habit of gnawing at herself.

Stub nails, grey hair, a sallow complexion and 20 pounds overweight. Sandy no longer felt attractive. The decline from her physical prime felt irreversible. Having kids destroyed her abdominal muscles and widened her hips by a foot and a half. Her breasts were sagged like water balloons and her destiny included jowls like her grandfather's. Prematurely decaying knees made her shuffle like an old woman. It would be her 55th birthday tomorrow, well beyond middle age. And on top of all that, she was still single, with little prospect of finding another life partner.

Sandy gave the sauce another stir and poured some red wine into a tumbler. She leaned against the sink, sipped and looked out the window to watch her neighbours. Across the street, Myrtle Edwards weeded her garden, straight-legged and bent at the waist like one of those plywood cutout lawn ornaments. Sandy no longer did her own yard work. After her marriage ended, she'd hired Smokin' Grass Lawn Care to maintain her property. Her yard was basic green. Functional and unadorned, it suited her.

Old Mrs. Anderson walked by with her rag-mop dog, a pink bow in its hair, tethered to her wrist. Mrs. Anderson waved to Myrtle with her left hand, which held a little green bag of poop. The sun shone and the temperature felt comfortable. Sandy wondered at what speed a car would need to hit a cement wall in order to ensure death.

A cloud passed in front of the sun, light shifted, causing Sandy to flinch as her mother's face appeared in the window. She blinked and realized it was her own reflection. She gulped more wine, then focused on her reflection, turned her jaw and ran her hand gently across the loose skin of her neck. She brushed away stray hair and turned back to the sauce. It had started to bubble.

She sighed, then gave the sauce a stir, and took another drink of wine. Turning toward the photos on the fridge, she smiled weakly at the miniature archive of her children's lives. Devon's high school graduation. Amber's prom. The three of them on the dock at the cottage. Images of Robert had been removed, her mother had never approved of him as a son-in-law. Found him too blue-collar, not good enough for Sandy.

Years had passed since any new pictures had been taken. Low self-esteem was embedded in the family's DNA. Sandy envisioned driving toward the bridge, on a sunny day just like this one. She would step on the gas to maximize impact. Just as she imagined her car about to hit the wall… the telephone rang. It startled her fantasy and accelerated her heart rate. She picked it up on the third ring. "Hello?"

"Hey Mom. What's happening? " It was her son, Devon, calling from the city. He sounded impatient, as always.

"Hi Dev. I'm just making—"

"Hey listen, I've had a change of plans and won't make it home this weekend."

"Oh, well, I—"

"Jack got some concert tickets, and I have a chance to go with him. So… I'll check in with you another time, eh?"

"Sure, thanks for—"

"No worries. Take it easy." And with a click the dial tone returned. Sandy replaced the receiver slowly, and gazed out the window. Devon attended a technical college in Toronto. He'd come home for Christmas holidays, but preferred to spend his time enjoying the delights of the big city. She chastised herself for wishing he had offered birthday greetings. Her children both had busy lives.

Amber worked as a flight attendant. Occasionally she had a layover in Toronto and sometimes called Sandy to meet for dinner. Her daughter had become unrecognizable compared to the photos on the fridge. When she graduated from high school, Amber took control of her compulsive eating, lost sixty pounds and had abdominoplasty surgery funded by her absentee father. She had recently been transferred to an international route. Amber had confided last year that she'd had a brief affair with a married pilot. The new schedule provided emotional space.

Sandy's keys were on the counter next to her glass of wine. She took another drink, then picked them up. The front door, the shed, the cottage, the car. She reconstructed her fantasy. As she ran her thumb over the car's ignition key she could picture turning it and putting the car in gear. She could feel the vibration in the soles of her feet and hear the pulse of the engine. In her imagination the engine sputtered… sputtered like a cartoon motor… then she realized it was the tomato sauce. She hurried over to the stove, grabbing oven mitts on her way, and took the pot off the heat. She'd ruined it. Burned it to the bottom of the pan. Her mother's judgmental voice scolded her for being inattentive. Sandy took a deep breath and began pouring the tomato sauce down the sink.

A waste of time… a waste of ingredients… a waste of space is how Sandy saw herself. Would anyone even notice if she disappeared? The doorbell's chime interrupted her self-loathing. She opened the door to find a florist deliveryman cradling a box in his arms. "I guess somebody loves you," he said, smiling. "I have a dozen yellow roses for you."

Confusion drowned her ability for coherent thought. She mumbled something unintelligible in response. Who could have sent her a birthday bouquet?

"Just sign here," requested the deliveryman. Then he passed her a clipboard bearing a pen.

Sandy removed the pen from its clip and prepared to sign. Her heart contracted as she scanned the document. "These are not for me."

"What do you mean, lady?"

"The address. It says 108 Meadowview Lane. My house is 103. See?" She handed the clipboard back to him.

"Oh shit! I mean... Sorry, lady. It's my mistake entirely."

"Don't worry," replied Sandy in a controlled voice. "Flowers make me sneeze anyway." She pasted a smile on her face and offered a little wave as the delivery van pulled away. Once it was gone she continued to stand on her porch, gazing at her car parked in the driveway. It crouched in the shade of the maple that dominated the property. She thought of fetching her keys and getting it over with.

Instead Sandy returned to the kitchen phone. She called Celeste; a friend she'd known since university. They had supported each other through life's challenges. Celeste was confident, decisive, everything Sandy felt she lacked herself.

"Hey, Celeste. How are you?"

"Sandy. I am *so* glad you called. I feel like shit, that's how I am."

"Oh. Gosh. What up?

"It's that horrid Lydia Hamilton. She thinks she runs the whole damn country club. Just because her husband is Chairman of the Board, doesn't mean *she* has any power. Does it?"

"Not really."

"Well, someone ought to tell her, because I'm getting sick and tired of watching her strut around like she's Queen Bee."

"Just ignore her."

"Ignore her! I'd like to run her over with my car. That's what I'd like to do."

"You know..."

"Seriously Sandy, you've seen her in action. The girls hang on her every word. Remember when Lydia threw a party the same night as Janice's just to draw people away. When Patti said she was going to buy a new Fiat, Lydia bought one first, she stole Wendy's pool boy, and… she asked me if I colour my hair."

"She did not."

"She did too!"

"Perhaps she just loved your beautiful shade of blonde."

"I don't know how you can defend her. Honestly, that woman makes my blood boil. But… enough about me. You just called to say hi and here I am dumping all my crap on you. What's up with you?"

"I'm fine. Just burned a batch of pasta sauce, but that's typical for me." Sandy poked at the pot reclining in her sink.

"You've never been strong on the domestic front. I don't know why you make the effort when it's just you. As soon as both of your kids moved out you should have switched to take-away menus and frozen entrees. You should sell that big old house, Sweetie. Your kids don't need you any more and you certainly have no sentimental memories of your time there with Robert. Move to a condo. Simplify. Make a change."

"Mmmm. A change."

"Hey, how's your mom. Have you been over to see her today?"

"No. I was there yesterday. She did her typical rant about the jail I put her in and how awful the food is. She made the kid who serves lunch cry and told me I brought the wrong flavour of Boost. Just a normal visit."

"She's a piece of work, your mom. Ooops. I'm getting another call. I've got to let you go, Sweetie. Let's catch up later. We can do lunch at the club next week and I'll fill you in on the next installment of the soap opera that is my life."

"Sure."

"Bye-bye," said Celeste.

Sandy listened to the dial tone and entertained a new fantasy. In this scenario she lived in a downtown condo with an open floor plan and high-end finishes. She pictured herself on the balcony, twenty pounds thinner, wearing a power suit and holding a glass of wine with dramatic red nails. She replaced the receiver and refilled her glass.

The clatter of her mailbox lid alerted her. She carried her drink to the front porch to retrieve the mail. Across the street Myrtle was now watering her flowerbeds. She used a watering can rather than a hose and wore a cotton sunbonnet. Myrtle looked like an ancient Holly Hobby doll as she waddled across her yard. Sandy brought the bundle of letters back to the kitchen and sat at the table.

The cable TV bill, VISA, a plea from a charity working with children in developing nations, a couple of store flyers, and a single personal letter. When Shirley saw the return address she drained her glass and reached for the near empty bottle.

She had applied to Smythe, Anderson, Brant and Associates in response to their ad on Workopolis. It took her three days to pull together a presentable resume. She had been employed as a legal secretary when fresh out of university, but as soon as they had kids, Robert insisted she stay home full-time. After Robert left, Sandy took a series of part-time or seasonal jobs in retail, as well as office temp positions. She wanted to keep busy, and rebuild her confidence more than generate income. Robert had been generous, but now that Devon and Amber were gone, the child support went with them. Sandy had to do something to keep herself afloat. The thought of returning to the intense world of corporate law appealed to her.

Sandy could not bring herself to open the envelope. Instead she refilled her wineglass and revisited her fantasy in the downtown condo. In her mind she was once again slim, in a perfectly tailored suit, and beautifully groomed. Getting this job would make all the difference for her. She took a sip and pried open the envelope.

The letter was concise and formal. They had selected another candidate whose credentials were a better match to the company's needs. They wished her success in her search. The interview had only lasted 20 minutes. She knew they wanted someone younger, with more recent experience. Someone decorative to accessorize their reception desk. She finished her drink, then sat with her elbows on the table and her head in her hands.

Sandy lost track of how long she remained in that position, until the fullness of her bladder commanded her to rise. When she returned from the bathroom, she realized it had become dark enough to require the kitchen lights, but she didn't bother to turn them on. The wine bottle was almost empty. Not even enough for a full glass remained, so Sandy drank it straight from the bottle's neck, then carefully placed it in the blue box along with three others.

She rinsed her glass and scrubbed the pasta pot, then put both away. She sponged tiny flecks of pasta sauce from the counter and stovetop, smirking to herself as she imagined how one would clean blood from a crime scene. She gathered the mail from the table, carried it to the den and shredded it. Returning to the kitchen, she carefully removed all the photos from the fridge and slipped them into her purse. She put the magnets in the junk drawer and admired the appliance's clean, brushed metal surface. Glancing around the kitchen Sandy tucked in the chair she had used and tore the page off the calendar. Even though it was only the 15th today, she preferred the look of the upcoming month, free of appointment notations. Sandy picked up her purse and keys then headed for her car.

Calmness possessed her. Sandy zig-zagged to the driveway, then shuffled around her car like a toddler at a coffee table. She settled behind the wheel, started the engine and reversed without looking into a blessedly abandoned street. Her neighbours gathered around dinner tables while Sandy headed for the Hamilton Street Bridge as if her vehicle was set to autopilot.

Oblivious to her surroundings, Sandy ran a stop sign without incident, changed lanes without signaling and cruised through a traffic light that had just turned red. Her mind floated in a meditative state, completely serene, until flashing lights and the chirp of a siren shocked her from her reverie. There was a police car behind her, clearly signaling her to pull over. She complied.

Sandy watched in her rearview mirror as a tall, male officer unfolded himself from the cruiser. He reached back and withdrew a cap that he placed on his head and adjusted. He pulled a small notepad from his breast pocket, approached Sandy's window, bent down and tapped on the glass with a pen.

Lowering the window, Sandy looked up at the Ken-doll constable. She was wide-eyed and speechless.

"Good evening ma'am. May I see your license and registration please?"

Sandy fumbled through her purse, and pawed her license from her wallet then let the wallet fall to the floor. Once she handed the license to the officer, she leaned over to the glove compartment and withdrew the little plastic folder with the ownership and insurance cards.

"Have you had anything to drink this evening, ma'am?" asked the officer in an unexpectedly gentle voice.

"Yes."

"Are you aware you went through a red light at the last intersection?"

"What?"

"Can you step out of the car please, Ms. Crewson?"

"Why?"

"Can you step out of the car for a moment, please, ma'am?" The officer stood and stepped back to allow Sandy to open her door. He had blue eyes, was young, maybe thirty, and looked impossibly tall from Sandy's perspective.

Sandy began to cry. Not just a sob, or a whimper to seek leniency. She bawled. Tears flooded down her face, her nose ran, and she couldn't catch her breath to speak. She looked up at the officer, who had raised one eyebrow, and it seemed that the torrent of tears escalated. Sandy wiped her runny nose on her sleeve and said, "I don't... I can't... I'm so sorry..." She dropped her forehead against the steering wheel and continued to weep.

Sandy had little recollection of being guided to the squad car. She was unaware of the care the officer took as he placed her in the rear seat, had no memory of the cellmates with whom she'd spent the night, but later realized her aborted plan became a positive juncture.

Adopt-a-Pet

Todd and Brittany were ready for an addition to their family. They snuggled on their champagne-coloured couch, custom ordered from Crate & Barrel, under a fringed ecru throw they had found at Home Outfitters. With their temples touching they admired the staging of their IKEA birch veneer bookcases. Touches of colour had been added through the tasteful placement of miniature vases and porcelain animals among the books, which had been carefully selected for their jacket tone or trendy titles. Their hearts were overflowing with love and gratitude, and their sprawling subdivision bungalow, with its ample fenced-in yard, had empty space that needed filling. Todd and Brittany had two solid years of wedded bliss under their belts, and they had been inspired to share their abundance in response to their friends' actions.

Last week their good pals, Brad and Amy, came over for burgers and beer. Brittany took pride in the fact no one could tell her homemade patties were tofu, and Todd had just picked up a new batch from the microbrewery across town. For the first half hour of the visit, the guests were enchanted by the beauty of Todd and Brittany's home. Brittany smiled as Amy used her phone to tweet pictures of the walk-in closet.

Once the foursome was seated outside, Bramy... as Brad and Amy like to be called, to demonstrate the strength of their partnership... Bramy just couldn't stop talking about the new puppy they had adopted from the Humane Society. It was a Shepherd/Collie mix and they had named him Tin-Tin. They said Tin-Tin came from a litter of eight. He had been born to a farmer who wanted to drown the puppies, but the farmer's wife delivered the unwanted litter to the Humane Society.

"Even so," said Brad, "the shelter staff planned to put him down by the end of the week if he wasn't adopted. We saved his life."

"Saved his very life," echoed Amy.

"You see, they can't afford to keep the dogs indefinitely. They eat more as adults and require more space," explained Brad.

"Bigger cages, and larger portions of food," clarified Amy.

"Besides, people are most attracted to puppies…"

"They're so cute!" inserted Amy.

"… and so that's the best time to have them adopted. If we had come three days later, Tin-Tin would have been dead," said Brad.

"Oh, don't say that, Brad. I can't bear the thought," pouted Amy.

Todd and Brittany made eye contact with raised brows. The thought of saving a life, and giving another creature a new chance appealed to them tremendously. However, it surprised them that Bramy were up to the task.

"It's like practicing to be a parent," Amy said. "We have to feed Tin-Tin and give him water to drink. We got a little bed for him at Pet World and he sleeps right in the corner of our master suite."

"He snores," added Brad.

"Snuffles, not snores," corrected Amy. "And we go to the park with Tin-Tin every day. We throw balls and Frisbees..."

"He doesn't catch them yet," said Brad.

"He's only a puppy. But he's learning to track where the ball goes, and he loves watching Brad bring it back." Amy beamed.

Bramy exchanged a look of adoration while Brad pulled out his cell phone. Todd and Brittany were treated to post-age-stamp photos of Tin-Tin looking at the camera with one folded ear and a tilt to his head. Tin-Tin sitting in the park. Tin-Tin looking out the car window. Tin-Tin beside his din-ner bowl. Tin-Tin sleeping in a patch of sunlight on Bramy's bed.

"Didn't you say he has his own bed?" asked Brittany.

"He does, but he loves *our* bed best," replied Amy.

"Can't stand to be away from us," added Brad. "We take him everywhere we can."

"Everywhere," agreed Amy. "Even the mall lets dogs in. We just have to say he's training to be a guide dog and then he can even come into restaurants with us."

"He loves McDonald's," said Brad. "Remember when I..."

"...knocked over your French fries," finished Amy.

"And Tin-Tin jumped up..."

"...and gobbled the whole thing in one gulp." Amy gig-gled.

Brittany wasn't keen on the idea of a dog in a restaurant, even if it was fast food, but Bramy were certainly finding pet care-giving to be a source of great joy. She would have liked to meet Tin-Tin, but Todd's allergies made it impossible for him to be near a dog. She wondered if Bramy realized Todd and Brittany would no longer be able to visit at their house. Even if the dog were locked outside, the home would be infested with allergens.

The next day Brittany met her best friend, Tiffany, at morning yoga class. After class Tiffany explained she had restructured her schedule to accommodate a new arrival in her household. "I'm a single mom," joked Tiffany. "A wonderful furry ball of happiness has come into my life. She has transformed my existence. She's a smoky Persian, with the cutest little pushed-in face, named Mrs. Wiggins."

Tiffany removed an elastic to release her blond hair and gave her head a playful shake. "I got her from the S.P.C.A. shelter. She has given new meaning to my life. After Theo and I broke up, I felt so lonely I thought I would die, but Mrs. Wiggins gives me all the love and affection I could ever want."

Tiffany showed Brittany the background image on her iPhone. "She cuddles on my lap and we eat Cheezies while watching chick-flicks."

"I remember you complaining that Theo never agreed with your choice of movies," said Brittany.

"And... I have a pink cotton pet sling that I got online for only $15.00. The only problem is I can't do yoga after work because I have to get right home and feed Mrs. Wiggins. As soon as I come through the door she waddles right up to me and demands dinner. She pushes her empty dish across the floor and scolds me for keeping her waiting. If I'm really late she'll make a little poop in the corner. It's adorable."

Brittany wasn't sure scolding and punitive pooping were desirable behaviours in a pet, but she held her tongue because Tiffany seemed so enthusiastic.

"I give her *Princess Pussy* feline stew, and a little bowl of milk, but not too much or she gets diarrhea. Then, after she's eaten I give her a good brushing. When she's been groomed she's so soft I could just eat her up."

Feeding a cat and eating a cat. Brittany smirked to herself, as she pictured Mrs. Wiggins in a wok. Just like Bramy, Tiffany had rescued Mrs. Wiggins from a shelter. The cat's previous owner had died, leaving the feline homeless. Mrs. Wiggins was not a kitten, but Tiffany said adopting an older animal is preferable because no training is required.

As she drove home from the yoga studio, Brittany fantasized about becoming a parent to some precious creature. The home she had created with Todd looked so beautiful, with far more space than the two of them needed. And love... they had more than enough love to share. She imagined the warm welcome she would receive when she returned from work. Bramy was right; it would be great practice for when she and Todd decided to have children. The only problem would be Todd's allergies.

That night Brittany searched the internet for information on non-allergenic pets. Although some sites listed names of dog breeds, most sources said no furry animal, not even a rodent like a guinea pig or hamster could be guaranteed to be allergy free. She did find a breed of hairless cat, but it was so boney and naked it looked like a character from *The Walking Dead*. She couldn't imagine cuddling with it. Anything with scales would be safe in terms of allergic reactions, but fish seemed boring, and reptiles gave her the creeps. She decided the best solution would be to put Todd on a regimen of allergy medications. She knew adoption would be the right thing for them.

The next step was to find a shelter. Brittany searched for locations near their home. The Humane Society was way across town, but a place called the Richardson Street Shelter seemed significantly closer. The best plan would be to take Todd to the shelter to see how he reacted to the potential adoptees, but when they arrived on Saturday, Todd expressed trepidation. "Do you really think we're ready for this? You know, once we've made a commitment we can't go back. It's not like returning a piece of clothing."

"We can do anything we put our minds to," Brittany said. She took Todd's hand and, on tiptoes, planted a kiss on his chin. "We have as much love to share as Bramy does, and our house is 500 square feet larger than theirs. Come on... you took the pill I gave you, right?"

The location Brittany had found was unfamiliar. Todd noticed, as he locked the Prius, that the buildings were in need of repair and he observed an alarming degree of litter. As they approached the shelter Todd saw a street person slumped on the pavement by the door. A mangled coffee cup with a few coins in it sat on the ledge beside him. Todd gathered the loose change from his pocket and tossed it in the cup, which startled the man awake. "Sorry... sorry... I just, uh, added some change to your collection," said Todd. He picked up his pace to catch up with Brittany.

At the shelter's reception counter, just a table in the foyer actually, Brittany was greeted by an elderly man with a hearing aid in each ear. He set aside the worn pocket book he had been reading and looked up at Brittany with faded blue eyes.

"Can I help you?"

"We're here to adopt," Brittany chirped.

"You're looking for who?" he asked.

"Well, not who, what," said Brittany.

"What?" he asked.

"Yes," said Brittany.

"Yes, what?" the man said with mounting frustration.

"Yes... what," asserted Brittany.

Todd stepped in to clarify the situation. "We have room in our home," he said. "We'd like to offer to take in... give a home to... well, you know, a needy creature." He and Brittany exchanged warm smiles and squeezed hands.

"Really?" the man asked.

"Yes," said Brittany. "We've thought a lot about it. We feel we are ready. We have the resources to take in a new family member."

"That's very generous of you," said the man, scratching the top of his balding head. "This is an unusual offer, but we are overcrowded, so a placement would really help. Did you have any specific requirements in mind?"

Todd and Brittany had discussed this very question in great detail. At first they had a lengthy list of physical attributes, personality traits, and size requirements, but in the end they had decided to leave it to chance. "We'll take the one in the greatest need," said Brittany.

At this the man rose slowly from his chair. It was clear that arthritis made movement difficult and he shuffled, rather than walked, down the hallway towards a back room. Through a security door, he led Todd and Brittany to a facility that looked very much like a hospital ward. Metal-framed single beds lined the side walls, and upon each reclined a scruffy elderly male. They looked to be in various stages of consciousness.

"Now Bob here…" the man began, gesturing to the second bed on the right.

"Wait a minute," said Todd. "These aren't animals."

"No, they certainly are not," said the man. "Although they have suffered many personal challenges, and have varying degrees of mental illness, these men are human beings and retain the dignity deserving to all of mankind."

"But, we thought…" Todd stammered.

"Can you excuse us for a minute?" asked Brittany. She pulled Todd aside to speak to him beyond the range of the man's hearing aids. "Don't you see what's happened?"

"What?"

"We've been given a higher purpose. Screw Bramy's Tin-Tin and Tiffany's Mrs. Wiggins. They're lower species. It is much more noble to adopt a real, live human being."

"What! You want to take one of these men home with us?"

"Just imagine the possibilities. We can clean him up; a shave, some new clothes. I've seen it on makeover shows. We'd have our very own grandpa. We could call him something cute, like 'Pappy.' You wouldn't be allergic, he wouldn't need any training, and he might even be able to help with chores around the house. We'd be the first to adopt a homeless person. We'd be adoption superstars."

And so, Todd and Brittany completed the paperwork that allowed them to add a new member to their family. Although Pappy's pungent aroma was a bit of a challenge on the trip home, he turned out to be quite docile and surprisingly photogenic. Todd and Brittany's tweets went viral.

High Tea for Two

Janice made the 1:00 reservation at The Huntington Hotel to beat the rush for high tea. She managed to secure a table for two on the patio shaded by an umbrella and over-looking the duck pond. When Sandy arrived, Janice rose and gathered her friend in a warm embrace lasting a little longer than either woman felt comfortable with.

"It is wonderful to have you home," said Janice. "I want to hear all about your adventure. I think you're so brave to go off by yourself. Meeting all those strangers... I couldn't do it."

"Nonsense," said Sandy as she laid her linen napkin across her lap. "You would have enjoyed the Sacred Goddess Focused Mind Retreat. It was a beautiful location."

"Good afternoon, ladies. My name is Ethan and I will be your server today. I understand you will be having our high tea?" The waiter leaned over the table to adjust the floral centerpiece.

"That's right. We want the full treatment." Janice beamed. "Oh... just a sec... I also have a gift certificate." She produced a crumpled rectangle of paper from her purse and passed it to the waiter. "Bring it on." Janice giggled.

"Excellent," he replied in a perfectly erect stance. "May I begin by telling you that here at The Huntington we pride ourselves on providing a classic English high tea. This is a Victorian tradition to help genteel ladies, such as yourselves, deal with the hunger gap between lunch and dinner."

"I purposely skipped lunch so I would be hungry," said Janice as she glanced at the servings in front of her fellow patrons.

"Wonderful," continued Ethan. "Our service includes a variety of gourmet finger sandwiches, warm scones with clotted cream and gelée, and an assortment of sweet pastries."

"Clotted cream? Just bring me a bowl and spoon," joked Janice as she squirmed. The café chair's rounded seat looked adorable, but her ample thighs hung over the edges. She adjusted the drape of her skirt so other patrons would be unaware.

"Let me start you with the tea," suggested Ethan. "What can I bring you?"

"What kinds do you have?" asked Janice.

"Well, would you like a black tea, green tea, white tea or herbal blend?" Ethan glanced over his shoulder at the foursome of grey-haired ladies being seated by the hostess.

"Is there something you could recommend?" Sandy asked. She repositioned the napkin in her lap and smoothed the floral tablecloth.

Ethan smiled. "Our teas are picked and prepared by hand at some of the most highly regarded plantations in China, Sri Lanka, India and Africa. The leaves are blended for us by world-renowned connoisseur Tabitha Cornwall-Howard. May I recommend our house blend? It has the flavourful depth of an English breakfast tea with a floral bouquet and satisfying complexity. It's a rich dark blend that includes a deep malt finish that's perfect without milk."

Janice and Sandy gazed at their waiter. The soft sheen of a black bow tie perched on top of a crisp white shirt with perfectly aligned petite black buttons, neatly tucked into pleated black Dockers with a patent leather Louis Vuitton belt. They would have ordered a pot of sewage sludge if he'd suggested it.

Once Ethan left, the two old friends returned to their chatter. Resting their elbows on the table, they both leaned in and dispensed with the obligatory updates about their children's activities and neighbourhood gossip. "Okay," said Janice. "What I really want to hear about is the Sacred Mind Goddess Retreat."

"Sacred Goddess Focused Mind Retreat," corrected Sandy.

"Isn't that what I said?"

Sandy smiled. "Well, it was a beautiful setting. A cluster of little cabins with a large dining hall in the centre. It used to be a children's camp, but has been renovated as a meditative retreat centre."

"You didn't have to use outhouses, did you?" asked Janice.

"The accommodations were modest, but modern. Each cabin had been designed to hold four people, with two sets of bunks and a shared washroom that had a shower. Due to our age, the top bunks weren't used. We stored our stuff there."

"I went to camp when I was a kid. Camp Wanna Haw Haw, located on a little lake near Huntsville. There were spiders in the cabins the size of hamsters, and the toilets and showers were in a communal building. We were all given yellow T-shirts with a picture of a laughing Indian on the front."

"Indigenous person," said Sandy.

"What?"

"Amber insists that the word 'Indian' is considered offensive. The politically correct term is indigenous person or aboriginal person," explained Sandy.

"If you ask me, the world's getting way too uptight about politically correct terms," said Janice. "I never know what to say anymore. It used to be no problem to say, He's a homo—"

"Your tea, ladies," said Ethan as he set the pot on the table between Janice and Sandy. He stiffly placed an antique china cup with saucer in front of each of them. Janice had a matched set with small pink flowers and a gold band along the rim, worn from years of use. Sandy's had blue flowers, but those on the saucer did not match the cup; a unique pairing caused by broken partners. Ethan placed a small silver tray holding crystal sugar and milk servers beside the teapot and then withdrew.

"So, who was your roommate?" asked Janice.

"Annika. She was a yoga instructor from Scarborough. She said she was 55, but she looked a lot younger than us. You know the kind, super flexible, lean, tight skin. She got up at sunrise every morning to do sun salutations on the lawn."

"Don't you just hate those kinds of people? They make you feel guilty about being normal," said Janice. "How long do we need to let this tea steep?"

"I don't know. Pour a little in your cup and see what it looks like."

Janice poured some tea into her cup. It was the golden colour of light maple syrup and did indeed smell like flowers. She filled both cups and added sugar to her own. Neither wanted to taint the exotic liquid by adding something as mundane as milk.

"So… what exactly did you do at this camp? Were you sitting cross-legged staring at your navels?" Janice laughed at her own wit. "Was there a guru? Incense?"

"Yes, we sat cross-legged, but we focused on breathing," said Sandy. "We were in search of selflessness through the understanding of inhalation and exhalation. Investigating the character of our breath allowed us to build our capacity for compassion."

"Really? You just breathed?"

"We aimed to purify our thoughts. We had to practice reining in our wandering minds and build our equanimity."

"Your what?"

"Equanimity. It means mental calmness or composure. The ability to maintain an evenness of temper, especially in a difficult situation," said Sandy.

"Hell, I've spent years perfecting my temper." Janice laughed, but noticed that Sandy did not join in. "So, you sat cross-legged and breathed and stayed calm?"

"That's right."

"And you did this for ten days?" Janice took a sip of her tea and looked at the adjacent table. "How much did it cost to learn how to breathe?"

Before Sandy could respond, Ethan arrived to present a three-tiered dish laden with miniature sandwiches. "Ladies, today's assortment of finger sandwiches includes shredded organic chicken from Summerset Farms with lemon and tarragon dressing on seven grain bread. There is Black Forest ham with celeriac rémoulade and tomato chutney on onion bread. Here you will see BC smoked salmon with brown shrimp butter and rock samphire on a light rye. Finally, we have a classic cucumber with crème fraîche and rocket greens on stone-ground white bread."

Janice and Sandy gazed, slack-jawed, at the edible sculpture the serving dish had become.

Ethan set a small plate in front of each woman. "Is there anything else I can get you ladies?"

"No," whispered Sandy. When he left she explained, "I've been starving for over a week. All we ate at the retreat was weed salads, raw vegetables, and birdseed bread. I don't know if my system will survive the richness of this."

"It is beautiful, isn't it?" said Janice as she started filling her plate with tiny sandwiches. "And this is only the first course." She noticed that her pinky finger instinctively extended as she placed each morsel on her plate.

Sandy lifted her small plate, amazed at the lightness of the delicate china. It had a single pink rose in the centre: a cobalt band interspersed with a variety of flowers formed an outer ring and a filigree gold edge completed the vintage pattern. "The biggest challenge at the retreat was trying to align our breath with our bodies," she said as she placed tiny sandwiches on her plate.

"What does that mean? Your breath is *in* your body, so how could they *not* be aligned?" asked Janice. A tiny dab of lemon tarragon dressing nestled in the corner of her mouth.

Sandy felt amazed at how the smoked salmon melted on her tongue. She made an effort to eat the miniature sandwiches in bites rather than succumb to the temptation of popping the whole thing into her mouth at once. "Mindfulness is the practice of paying attention to what is going on in the present. Instead of letting past errors or anger taint a current experience, you focus on what is happening in the now. It's important not to worry about the future either. Just enjoy the present."

Janice knew Sandy was referring to her own divorce and D.U.I. conviction, but decided to keep the conversation light. "What about happy memories, or planning events?" Janice refilled both teacups with a liquid that approached molasses in colour. This time she added both sugar and milk.

Ethan appeared. "Is everything to your satisfaction, ladies?"

"Everything is delicious," said Sandy.

"Almost ready for the warm scones?" asked Ethan.

"Just a sec," said Janice as she placed the last two sandwiches on her plate. "Now we are." She smiled up at Ethan, who lifted the tiered dish and headed toward the kitchen.

"Fondly remembering the past, or making plans for the future, are not the issues that need to be addressed," said Sandy. "The problem was my constant analysis of my broken marriage. Replaying past events negatively impacted my health and enjoyment of life. The mindfulness practitioners taught us to monitor our thoughts, feelings, behaviour and physiological status. We learned to step outside ourselves for our own well-being."

"Step outside of yourselves? You mean like astral body projection? I read a lot about that in high school. I used to think I would like to travel outside of my body, fly around the world, spy on people." Janice ate another sandwich. "If I got out of this body now, I think I'd be looking for a better one to get into." She laughed and shifted on the uncomfortable little chair.

"There's an example of how mindfulness could help you, Janice. You are always saying how unhappy you are with your appearance. Judging from how often you say it aloud, you must say it to yourself ten times more often. Mindfulness helps you become aware of that voice in your head so you can focus on it."

"Focus on it?" Janice tucked the last sandwich into her mouth and continued speaking while she chewed. "Why would I want to focus on the voice in my head telling me I'm fat?"

"Well..." Sandy felt as if preparing to step off a cliff. "If you have a voice in your head saying that... you could focus on telling it to shut up because you're perfect as you are, or..."

"Or?" Janice swallowed the sandwich and drained her tea.

"Or, you could listen to it and take some positive action."

"Here we go, ladies," said Ethan as he placed a basket covered with a linen napkin on the table. "Fresh out of the oven. I have brought you both plain and raisin scones, baked to a golden perfection. This is Cornish clotted cream, imported from the UK, and Marco Polo gelée, flavoured with flowers from Tibet. Enjoy."

Janice and Sandy remained still, the words *positive action* ringing in their ears, until laughter at the next table broke the spell. "Mmmm. They smell delicious," said Sandy.

"It would be a shame to let them go cold," said Janice. She carefully lifted the napkin to reveal a golden crust peppered with raisins. "Do you put on the cream first or the jam?"

"I think the gelée goes first, and the cream is a sort of topping," said Sandy.

The duo fell into silence as they broke open the warm scones and applied the sweet toppings. Ethan delivered a second pot of tea, refilling both cups before he departed. After they each devoured two scones, one of each type, the women settled back in their chairs with a sigh.

"Just then I was being very, very mindful," said Janice. "I totally focused on how fabulous those scones were, how sweet the jam tasted and how the cream melted."

"And I'm aware of how full my bladder is," said Sandy. "Where's the washroom?"

After Sandy returned, Janice made the trip to the restroom. Getting up to move felt good. When Janice returned to the table, the empty basket and dregs of the cream and gelée had been removed. She scanned the restaurant in the hope of spotting a seat cushion, but no such item was visible. She wondered why a backside as padded as hers did not offer more protection from the uncomfortable chair, asked herself if the previous thought had been the unfocused voice Sandy had spoken about, then told herself that noticing the pain in her butt seemed very mindful. Thinking about thinking confused her.

Janice smiled at the ladies at the next table, who seemed very interested in her return. She smoothed the drape of her dress and turned to her companion. "So, it sounds like you had a fabulous experience at the Focused Goddess Mind Retreat."

"That's Sacred Goddess Focused Mind Retreat," said Sandy.

"Are you going back next year?" Janice asked.

"No."

"No?"

"No."

"Why not? It sounds like you learned a lot. You said it was a beautiful place. Was the food that awful? Was it too expensive? Did your roommate bother you?"

"Which question would you like me to answer?" Sandy smiled.

"What the heck is that?" said Janice. Her eyes were focused just past Sandy's right shoulder.

"I have pastries for you, ladies," said Ethan as he stepped up to the table. He set down a silver tray, lined with an intricate paper doily, under a delicate stack of beautiful pastries. "Our feature fruit pastry today is a blueberry puff, there's a petite chocolate croissant, our house version of a Victoria sponge and to complete the quartet the chef's special mini peanut butter cheesecake."

"Oh my," said Janice. She shifted on the chair. She wondered if she could start carrying around one of those orthotic seat cushions. They seem socially acceptable.

"May I suggest, to accompany your sweets, a Darjeeling tea? It is considered to be the champagne of teas. Darjeeling is best enjoyed with a light infusion of milk. It has significantly softer tannins, which offers a perfect balance for the sweet pastries."

"Yes, please," whispered Sandy.

Ethan cleared away the pot, used cups and dishes, while the friends sat in silence taking in their quaint surroundings. He returned promptly with a hot teapot and new vintage cups and saucers. This time Sandy had a matched set with a pale blue edge, vibrant rose clusters and gold accents on the rim, foot and handle. Janice's had a soft pink cup, with white polka dots and a flower inside. "Enjoy, ladies." Ethan turned and spoke to the next table, causing those women to giggle.

"So, you were saying that you don't want to go back. Did something happen?"

"Not really," said Sandy.

"Not really' is not the same as 'No'," countered Janice. "Talk to me."

"Well…" Sandy took a deep breath and exhaled slowly.

"Are you being mindful?" Janice asked with a smile.

"Okay, here's the story. Every day we would meditate in the morning. Like I said, we sat cross-legged and we breathed. In the afternoons we had workshops, sort of mini-lectures, and in the evenings we did yoga."

"Sounds like a full day. You ready for some champagne tea?" Janice poured the amber liquid with a spicy aroma. She added sugar to hers and they both topped their cups with milk. Janice and Sandy locked eyes for a moment, then each placed a sweet on their plates.

"I found it to be a pleasant schedule. Not hectic, well paced. There was time to decompress, but always something interesting ahead. Then, on the fourth night, during the yoga session, I farted."

"You what? Oh my god. How awful! Did everyone hear it?" Janice brought her hands to her cheeks. "Oh no. Did they all turn and look at you? Did they laugh? Oh, Sandy. How awful for you. How did you manage to face them?" Shame triggered her.

"Calm down. It was fine. People giggled. The instructor explained that yoga poses jostle your organs and the release of internal gases is normal. It was fine. People carried on."

"You poor thing."

"There's more. The next night the same thing happened, only, I swear it sounded louder. People tried not to laugh, but honestly, it was like a whoopee cushion."

"Was it something you ate, Sandy? Maybe green vegetables or something? Too much soda perhaps? Are you going to eat the other peanut butter cheesecake?"

"No, go ahead, and no, it wasn't something I ate."

"Then what made you fart so much?"

"Are you enjoying the Darjeeling?" Ethan hovered over the women like an archangel. "Can I get you anything else, ladies?"

"It is lovely, thank you," said Sandy

"We're just going to relax and digest for a bit, if that's okay," added Janice.

"Certainly. Give me a wave when you're ready." He left to attend to other patrons.

"So, what did you do? Did you ask to be excused from further yoga sessions? I would have. They can't *make* you participate in any of their activities. You were there by your own choice. You had the right to decide not to do yoga if you were being humiliated. Or the instructor should have chosen different poses. Or *he* could have farted, so it wasn't only you."

"Don't be ridiculous, Janice."

"I'm not. The staff at those places are supposed to make people feel better. We should write a letter of complaint. You don't have to put up with this, Sandy."

"I toughed it out, kept to the back of the room and took it easy whenever he gave us a twisting pose. I clenched my cheeks and everyone pretended they heard nothing. I felt embarrassed, but it wasn't life-threatening."

"Well, farting in yoga class is embarrassing, but that's nothing compared to what happened to me." Janice accentuated her point with a wave of her arms.

"Really?"

"Last Christmas at Trevor's company party I ate the spinach dip. You know the one. It's made in a hollowed-out loaf of pumpernickel."

"Right."

"I love that stuff, but whoever made it did not blend the spinach very well and a chunk got caught in my front tooth. No one told me, so I spent half of the party looking like a hillbilly with a missing tooth."

"Are you ready for the bill, ladies?" Ethan stood beside their table with a slip of paper and a portable debit terminal. After some fussing over who would pay, Janice dealt with the bill and the women departed.

Following Sandy towards the exit, Janice suggested, "You know, maybe we should go to the Goddess Retreat together next year. You look like you lost a couple of pounds." She trailed after Sandy, weaving her way through the tables towards the exit. Janice noticed heads turn as she passed. She was unaware that during her visit to the washroom her skirt's hem had gotten tucked into her Spanx.

Marion Reidel

Double Chocolate Toffee Delight

Celeste could feel the sugar invade her bloodstream the moment she swallowed.

"Do you like it? I've never tried this recipe before. I found it online and thought it sounded absolutely delicious. I couldn't resist giving it a try. It's called Double Chocolate Toffee Delight. There's a calorie-reduced version, but I decided to go for the authentic option." Janice was nearly bouncing with excitement, and waved the serving spatula like a wand as she spoke.

Celeste wondered if it would sound rude to ask for a sip of water. Make that a tumbler. She raised a finger to indicate a response was forthcoming, then attempted to mentally trigger her salivary glands in the hope of rinsing away the goo that seemed to have sealed her lips.

"I really value your opinion," Janice continued. "I know you don't actually cook yourself, but you always hire the best caterers and so I know your taste is impeccable. Ha! Taste! That's a bit of a joke, isn't it? I meant your judgment, but we're talking about food so there's one of those double intentions."

Celeste smiled and nodded her head. She set her fork gently on the edge of Janice's Corelle plate and mimed a signal for a drink.

"Oh, you want some water? Of course. It's a tiny bit rich." Janice hustled over to her large brushed metal side-by-side and took out a jug of filtered water in which floated slices of lemon. She removed a glass from the cupboard beside the sink and noticed food debris was stuck to the inside. The second glass she chose seemed worse.

"Just a sec. My dishwasher really doesn't do the job it should," Janice explained as she rinsed the glass. "I've tried those little detergent pillows with the power ball ingredient and a super sparkle rinse agent, but there's still bits of food left behind. My mother says it's because I don't scrape and rinse the plates, but I think if I have to do that, what's the point of having a dishwasher. Right?"

Celeste stifled a gag as she watched Janice polish the glass and set it on the counter next to the jug.

"I've always been of the opinion that appliances are here to make my life easier. It's not my responsibility to make their work easier." Janice chuckled as she dried her hands and dropped the crumpled linen tea towel on the counter.

Celeste began to feel light-headed. Her increased blood sugar level made her temples throb and vision lose focus. She pointed at the empty glass.

"Did you want ice?" asked Janice.

Celeste shook her head, maintaining what she hoped was the same pleasant smile, although she feared it had become a grimace.

"My homeopathic practitioner says we should all be drinking room temperature water," explained Janice as she lifted the jug and held it poised over the glass. "She says chilled water shocks the internal organs, but I still seem to crave the icy cold feeling of refrigerated water. Don't you?"

Celeste nodded and tried to resist holding her breath. She could feel sweat breaking out on her forehead. Janice filled the glass and handed it to her friend. As Janice turned to place the jug back in the fridge Celeste gulped half of the glass, and gave her chest a pound with her fist.

"So, what do you think of my Double Chocolate Toffee Delight?"

"My goodness, Janice, it's… very chocolatey."

"Exactly! That's the whole point. I read a blog post the other day that said eating chocolate improves your sex life." Janice placed a piece of the cake on a plate for herself. "How often do you and Charles have sex?"

Celeste gasped and felt her face flush. "That's a bit of a personal question, isn't it?" She picked up her fork, looked at the cake and set the fork down again.

"Well, I guess it's not really a question of hard numbers. What's often enough for one person might be too often for someone else. Right?" Janice took a bite of the cake and continued speaking as she swallowed. "Chocolate contains pheny-lethy-lamine, and that stuff releases dopamine, which then stimulates the pleasure centre of the brain, which triggers orgasms."

"Really?" Celeste shifted in her seat and checked the buttons down the front of her blouse. She took another drink of water.

"Yes, really. Research has shown that women who eat chocolate regularly, become sexually aroused more easily and achieve greater sexual satisfaction." Janice took a large bite of cake. "Did you know the Mayans and Aztecs thought cocoa was the food of the gods?" Janice used the back of her hand to wipe icing from the corner of her mouth.

"That's interesting," replied Celeste.

"Did you ever see that Johnny Depp movie?"

"Which one?"

"I think it was called *Chocolate*. This gypsy woman comes to a French village and opens a chocolate shop and makes all these wonderful treats that are aphrodisiacs. She makes chocolate with spices in it, and serves thick hot chocolate drinks. The Mayans invented hot chocolate, you know."

"No, I didn't." Celeste toyed with her fork, wondering how she might avoid eating the serving before her. The waistband of her pencil skirt felt tight just looking at the cake.

Janice continued to speak as she devoured half of her portion. "Chocolate is like a drug that offers excitement, euphoria and contentment. The blog said it has a positive psychological as well as biological impact on a woman's sexuality." She sighed. "Trevor and I have sex semi-weekly."

"I beg your pardon."

"That's twice a week." Janice dragged the index finger of her right hand through the thick layer of icing, inserted it between her puckered lips and made slurping sounds when she sucked on the finger as she withdrew it. She licked her lips and smiled. "Yep. On Sunday mornings, when we return from church, and on Wednesday nights. Regular as clockwork."

Celeste took a modest forkful of cake and held it poised above her plate. "Did the researchers say anything about these chocolate eating women putting on so much weight no one wants to have sex with them, or how they die from heart attacks?"

"Sex is good cardiovascular exercise," quipped Janice. She finished her last bite of cake and rose to take the plate to the sink. "And another thing, seems as we're confiding, it occurs to me that you subscribe to the North American definition of beauty far too rigidly."

"What do you mean?"

"Well, look at you. You're rake-thin and you still work out every single day."

"That's how I keep rake-thin." Celeste set down her fork and crossed her legs.

"There are lots of cultures that celebrate the beauty of a more curvaceous female form," said Janice as she placed her plate in the sink.

"Really?"

"In the Tonga Islands, Tahiti and Fiji, large women are considered the most desirable, like the ancient Venus carvings. And in the Middle East, carrying extra weight is seen as a sign of prosperity and robust health. A woman with a little meat on her bones is considered to be more fertile than skinny girls. And you know, women of African descent are considered most attractive if they have wide hips and ample booties." Janice turned and smacked her backside with a chuckle. "Being a large person is often associated with being a happy person. Just as eating chocolate makes people happy."

"Do you have a Tupperware container?" Celeste asked.
"Sure."

"I wonder if I could take this cake home with me. I think I need more time to digest both it and the information you've shared." She gently adjusted the fork on the side of the plate and smiled at her hostess.

"Sure thing." Janice went to the cupboard to get a container, then used Celeste's fork to slide the cake into the plastic box. Janice avoided eye contact with her slim friend. "I hope I haven't offended you, Celeste."

"Of course not. You've clearly given this matter a lot of thought." Celeste felt proud of her own trim physique and often felt Janice's bubbly personality overcompensated for her obese figure. "Good friends should be able to speak freely. Don't worry about a thing."

"Good," said Janice with relief. "I feared you thought I was bragging because I am having more sex than you are." Janice snapped the lid on the container and handed it to her friend with a grin.

Let's Pretend

The left side of Angela's forehead had a diagonal gash, brain matter projected like stuffing from a slashed cushion and blood dripped from the corner of her mouth. She thought she looked fabulous. She applied a layer of black lipstick, then reached for the long grey wig.

It had been 16 years since Angela attended a costume party. In fact, she could only remember one such event. When she was ten, in grade five at The Reformed Church of Jesus' Holy Name Elementary School, she had worn a witch costume to class. It was her first year of public education, having finally convinced her mother that home schooling was inhibiting her social development. The outfit had been a playful rendering of the classic fairytale archetype. Angela's green face make-up was topped by a striped, wide brimmed, pointed hat. She had been sent to the office immediately upon her arrival.

The Vice Principal thought Angela's costume was a celebration of Satanic values. "You look like a child from the dark side, evil spawn, a demon," he said. "This is yet another example of your inability to make good choices Miss Hooper. Since you are unable to conform to acceptable standards, I have no choice but to send you home for the day." As she sat in the office reception area, waiting for her mother, a parade of Disney princesses, comic book superheroes, and cartoon characters passed through the foyer.

Now, straggly grey hair draped over the shoulders of her bloodied, torn gown. As she assessed herself in the bedroom's full-length mirror, Angela dropped one shoulder, threw out the opposite hip and curled her left hand to her chest with fingers hooked. She wanted to be one of the walking dead.

Steve would pick her up in forty minutes. Angela touched-up the blood dripping down her jaw. She tightened the lid on the tube of fake blood, then dropped it into the small burlap sack that would serve as her purse. She added a package of breath mints that she'd set out on her bathroom counter. Angela had been dating Steve for three months, but this would be the first time she would meet his friends. Her stomach grumbled and she had to pee for the third time in the last ninety minutes.

She met Steve at work. Angela handled front-line reception at a large real estate firm specializing in high-end properties. Her role gave her ample opportunity to scout potential targets. Steve was the top performing sales agent. He stood 6' 2" with a carefully curated beard and custom made suits. Office gossip suggested he often slept with clients; sealed the deal in a very personal way. Angela accessed pay role information and discovered Steve earned a consistent six-figure income. Any woman could overlook a little philandering if it meant an affluent lifestyle. Steve had recently turned 30 and Angela felt sure he'd be ready to settle down soon.

For two months, Steve whisked by Angela's desk with a cheery, "Morning," but not even a sideways glance. She knew a man of Steve's status needed an executive assistant for a wife. So, she implemented a capture strategy.

As she continued to touch up her make-up Angela's bedazzled cellphone chirped for her attention. A glance at the screen informed her that mother was calling. She tapped speaker and continued adjusting her wig. "Hey Janice."

"Angela, Sweetie, how are you?"

"I'm fine. What do you need?"

"What makes you think I need anything? Can't I just call to say hello? You know it's important to me to stay connected."

Angela tuned out as her mother launched into a monologue about the trials and tribulations of her suburban life. Something about firemen and bathing suits, scones, it was the usual belch of unrequested information. Angela tolerated these intrusions out of guilt. She had left home when she became pregnant at 17. An act of rebellion against the sheltered upbringing she had received as Janice and Trevor Hooper's only child. It had been a disastrous decision. The boyfriend turned out to be an unreliable petty thief and she miscarried the baby at 3 months. It took Angela over a decade before she had the courage to contact her parents. By then she had put herself through secretarial school and had established a respectable life. She had taken to using their first names, couldn't bring herself to refer to them as mom and dad. Her mother misconstrued this as an act of friendship.

"Look, Janice, I don't have time for this now. I've got a costume party to go to. I'll come by next weekend."

"Great. Maybe we can go shopping. The outlet mall is having a big sale and I've got a 50% off coupon for lunch at Mama's Italian Kitchen."

As her mother continued detailing the plans for their future, Angela turned her blow dryer on and off above the phone a couple of times. She pressed the icon to disengage. "Technology is so unreliable," she told her reflection.

Angela rifled through her bedside table and found a package of strawberry flavoured condoms. She checked the expiry dates and tore off a strip of three. Her mother had forced her to attend Girl Guides. Angela learned one should always have a plan. She stashed the condoms in her bra.

A smile caused the blood on her chin to crack. Angela was proud of how she'd maneuvered Steve's affection. She tossed compliments towards him each time he passed. "Great haircut. That colour looks fabulous on you. Delicious cologne. Have you been working out?" She noticed an imaginary stain on his tie moments before he had to meet an important client, and just happened to have the perfect replacement in her desk. She brought him his favourite latte on the pretext that she had a two-for-one coupon. On Mondays bought cookies from the patisserie near her building, microwaved them at work to replicate fresh baked goodness and set them out on her counter when she saw Steve's car pull into the lot.

Her attire took a turn towards sexy as she had her hemlines raised and purchased more revealing necklines. She removed Steve's mail from his inbox so that she could deliver it personally to demonstrate her competence by saving him from another mailroom mix-up. Leaning over his desk, she dangled her delights like a red cape in front of a tortured bull. When Angela's assistance with a late-night deadline turned into a sexual escapade on Steve's desk, she had him hooked.

The lobby buzzer announced Steve's arrival. He'd told Angela he would be dressed as a vampire. Her zombie costume had been intended to be a perfect Gothic match. She slumped into her walking dead pose and checked herself one last time before she lurched to open the door.

She stopped breathing as she absorbed the image of her statuesque date. Steve was not dressed in the classic manner of Bela Lugosi, nor had he adopted the persona from Nos-feratu. He chose to be a romantic Vampire, like Anne Rice's Lestat. He looked like Tom Cruise. His velvet jacket with lace cuffs topped satin pantaloons and patent leather shoes. She stammered, "Y-you... ah... look... pretty."

Steve drove to their destination in nearly complete silence. He simply grunted in response to Angela's burbling. "When you said vampire, I pictured old school scary. I guess I have a tendency toward Gothic rather than romantic."

"Mmmm."

"I just wanted to have a costume that matched yours. Actually, this is kind of funny. We're sort of like salt and pepper. You know? It's a bit of a twist."

"Uh-ha."

"Usually the girl would be beautiful and the guy creepy. You know. It's really sort of funny that we've reversed it. I think it's funny. Don't you? I think people will be amused."

"Mmmm." Steve did not take his eyes off the road.

The hostess, a blonde, Disneyesque princess with a perfect complexion, greeted them. "Steven! Don't you look good enough to eat?" She licked her lips in what Angela thought was a most unprincess-like manner. "And this must be Andrea. It's so nice to meet you. Steve's told us all about you. It's so nice to finally meet you. It's almost like he's been hiding you from us."

The princess let out a sparkle of laughter before Angela could correct her name. The laugh sounded like glass wind chimes, light but potentially dangerous. Angela felt a strong desire to vomit.

Immediately upon entrance Steve disappeared toward the bar and managed to elude Angela's company throughout the evening. She caught glimpses of him as he wove his way past the naughty nurses and sexy police officers who were accompanied a variety of bare chested pirates and spandex encased superheroes.

Steve suggested an early departure. Muttered something about a migraine. Angela's attempts to apologize during the return trip were quashed with, "Don't worry about it," and "It's nothing." Steve declined a goodnight kiss due to potential make-up transference. His costume was rented.

Back in her bedroom Angela disrobed and removed her wig. Instinctually, she pulled out her phone and pressed *mom*. "Hey there, it's me."

"Hi Sweetie, how did the party go?" asked Janice.

"Fine. I got home earlier than expected and thought I'd check on you. I'm sorry we got cut off before."

"You need to get a better phone."

"So, shall I come over this Saturday and we'll use the lunch coupon?"

"That'd be great, Honey. Why don't you pick me up at 11:00?"

"Sounds good." Angela looked in the mirror as she spoke. She began to wipe the dark circles from beneath her eyes. "And then we can hit the outlet mall. I'm due for a wardrobe revision. I think Women's World is having a big sale."

"That's super, Sweetie. Listen, I'm watching a movie."

"Oh yea? What are you watching?"

"That one about the guy with the mask. He keeps killing people. I gotta go, he's about to kill the girl." Janice disconnected.

As the shower warmed up Angela once again assessed

herself in the mirror. Fake blood smeared with the white skin make-up, which ended at her collarbone. She removed her tattered gown to step into the shower and noticed her left breast was embossed with a circular indent from the package of strawberry condoms.

Marion Reidel

I Saved Someone's Life

I know what you're thinking. "Celeste, *you* saved a human life?"

I once took a class to lower my stress level. Every Thursday night for two months we gathered for an hour in a church basement, sitting on thin yoga mats in spandex attire that should only be worn by people with less than four percent body fat. The instructor was an aged hippie who spoke about releasing negative energy and casting worries to the wind. She had us imagine writing our stress triggers on paper, then envision tearing the page and tossing it into a fire. She circulated through the room exposing our serene faces to the musky smoke of a smoldering bundle of dried weeds. All the while exotic chants were playing on a boombox and our leader hummed along in a nasal manner. I had paid the $125.00 fee in advance, so I attended all eight sessions.

I thought of this training on the day of... the incident. That day, stress already hung on me as if a lead blanket had been laid across my shoulders. I needed to buy a gift card for Lydia Hamilton. She serves on the *Always Helping Others League*, of which I am the new president. I have held that position since April, when the previous chair suffered a disfiguring facelift leaving her housebound for six months. Her misfortune created an open door that I just had to slip through, but Lydia Hamilton held the vice presidency and was not at all pleased when I wheedled my way into the lead role. She had been circling like a vulture, waiting for me to take a misstep. Yet, last week, when I forgot to bring copies of my carefully prepared agenda, Lydia offered to print out the items on the white board so the meeting could proceed. This suspicious act of kindness needed to be addressed promptly, so I headed downtown to get a gift card from the Bon Appétit Bistro, which is getting rave reviews from everyone at the club.

I was under a time constraint because I had a lunch date with Sandy Crewson-Wells. I always thought her hyphenated surname had a lovely rhythm to it, but, unfortunately, she's just Sandy Crewson once again. Sandy and I have been best friends since university. Together we got our degrees, achieved womanhood and snagged our husbands. That had been 30 years ago and my life has been chugging along very nicely since then. Sandy has had a bumpier path and it has always been my job to rush to her aid whenever a new crisis arose. We had supported each other through the challenges of finding nannies, dealing with interior decorators, and organizing themed birthday parties. The worst, of course, was when Sandy's husband decided to be gay. Sandy's been on her own for 13 years now. What an unlucky number. During that time, she had been too busy with her rebellious teenagers and returning to the work force to even fantasize about a new relationship. When she called to invite me to lunch, however, she suggested a change was in the wind. My stomach felt so knotted you'd have thought *I* was going on a first date. So, you can understand why I felt distracted that morning.

I was dressed in my floral summer shift and had on my sparkly sandals. They pinch my feet, but I wasn't walking too far and the wedge heels make my calves look positively sculptural. I had the gift card in my purse and stood at the light waiting to cross to the bookstore when… the incident happened. You see, I had to get a greeting card to put the gift card in. I needed something with a suitable image. I knew the image had to be something floral, because Lydia Hamilton is an avid gardener. I thought a blank card would be best. I would Google an insightful saying about gratitude and hand write it. I still have my nib pens and ink from the calligraphy course I took last spring. Nothing is more personal than a handwritten note.

Anyway, as I waited to cross the street I looked around and noticed an elderly lady staggering. I mean really, mid-morning and she already looked drunk. It was a disgrace and I was thinking about how the mental cases and maniacs that litter downtown should be put away somewhere, you know, get them off the street so the patrons at the bistro's outdoor tables don't see them, when suddenly… she tipped over. It wasn't a slow collapse, like a faint, or a land-on-your-butt sort of topple. She went over backwards without any indi-cation of trying to soften her fall and she smacked the back of her head on the sidewalk. She did not make a sound, no yelp of pain, but I did see something white go flying from her head and I thought to myself, "Wow, she's banged her head so hard she's knocked a tooth out."

Just then, the light changed and I was about to cross to the bookstore except I noticed no one had moved to check on the old gal and I realized I happened to be the closest person to her. So, naturally, I approached her prone body. I had to take care as I knelt beside her. My floral dress has a cream back-ground and a filthy sidewalk was the last place I wanted to kneel. The woman looked perfectly relaxed there on the side-walk, so I decided the best thing to do would be to call 9-1-1 and get her some professional help. I pulled out my phone and started to dial when a young woman rushed off a city bus that had parked at the curb and came running over to the old gal, whom she called Ethel. It turned out they were neigh-bours. As I looked up to see the young woman approaching, I noticed the bus driver on a phone, so I assumed my 9-1-1 call would be redundant. I put my phone away, because now I had *two* people in crisis to deal with: Ethel, who seemed the picture of relaxation on the sidewalk, and her young friend, who was screaming at Ethel, asking if she was all right.

Have you ever noticed how, when you're in a crisis situ-ation, things move in slow motion? I had time to remember sitting on that yoga mat and could even smell the musky in-cense. I decided I had to take charge if Ethel was going to survive. When I attended school I took a first aid class and I was amazed to discover I could recall the steps to be taken. First, I had to speak to the person and see if they needed help. Well, my young companion had done that and from what I witnessed I was pretty sure Ethel would appreciate some as-sistance even though she declined to respond. We were also trained to keep everyone calm and talk to the victim in a clear authoritative manner. I am very good at taking charge. So, I said to the young woman, "Ethel is fine. She's had a bit of a fall, but help is on the way." Then I noticed the white thing that had flown from Ethel's head was not a tooth but a faux pearl earring. I mean, really it had to be faux, didn't it? Anyway, in order to give my young companion a purposeful task I pointed out the stray earring and suggested she put it in Ethel's purse because Ethel would not want to lose it. The young woman did this immediately and I felt I had the situation well in hand.

The next thing I remembered from those long-ago first aid lessons was the recovery position. I recalled that you don't want to leave the victim on their back because if they throw up, as a result of the trauma, then they could choke and die. This is a piece of information that I had used many times at university parties when alcohol consumption had laid someone out. So, my young companion and I gently rolled Ethel on her side facing towards the young woman on the opposite side from me. I immediately regretted this decision because the back of Ethel's head was soaked in blood and the skirt of my sundress lay perilously close to touching her.

I decided the next thing required was direct pressure on the wound, to stem the flow of blood. The problem was, what to use? I looked over at the bus driver, still in his seat talking on the phone, and realized not as much time had passed as I had thought. My companion had nothing to offer, nor did I, and so perhaps I appeared to be frozen and confused for just a moment.

To my left, a handsome young man started undressing. I have crystal-clear recollection of this. Over six feet tall, he was a slim twenty-something who towered over me as I crouched on the pavement. He unzipped his hoodie with what appeared to be seductive slowness, and then peeled off his T-shirt to reveal a hairless tanned chest and abs tight enough to bounce a ball off. My momentary paralysis was broken when the young man handed me his shirt.

As I pressed the T-shirt against Ethel's wound, I hoped the young man had showered that morning. At this point,

Ethel started to moan and Ethel's friend expressed delight and relief. I could hear sirens approaching, so I looked up to see a fire truck pull to the curb. It was with great pleasure I stepped aside to let the first responders come to Ethel's aid. I rose, and admired the efficiency of their work while holding my bloodied hands out so as not to smear my dress. At that point a handsome firefighter called me over to the truck. I felt sure he would commend me on my quick reaction and ability to remain calm, but instead he handed me a container of baby wipes and held out a pump bottle of sanitizing gel.

He said, "You shouldn't touch other people's blood, lady."

I wondered if he expected me to have latex gloves in my purse at all times. Ha! Anyway, I cleaned up my hands, taking care to get under my nails and around the cuticles. I had no cuts so I assured myself my heroic behaviour would not result in contamination.

As an ambulance arrived I finally crossed the street and found a card for Lydia Hamilton. I paid for it, then I realized my hands were shaking and so I explained to the clerk, "I am a little distraught. I had to save someone's life just now… out on the street. The emergency vehicles are still there."

The café where I'd arranged to meet Sandy was a block down the street, still within easy sight of the trucks and flashing lights. My goodness, they were taking a long time to get poor old Ethel to the hospital. I used the restaurant's washroom to scrub my hands, feeling a bit like Lady Macbeth. When Sandy arrived, she wasn't particularly interested in hearing my tale. I decided there was no need for me to be the focus at that moment. I graciously gave Sandy my attention because I realized a time would come when I could begin a conversation with, "I saved someone's life," and I'd have an audience hanging on my every word.

Marion Reidel

Viking Cruise

Myrtle dreamed of prying Frank out of the house. Since they retired eight years ago, her husband's only interests were found on the Golf Channel, the History Network and the Public Broadcasting Service. From his recliner he could watch a perfect swing, see the results of a WWII bombing strike or hear kitchen staff gossip in an Edwardian mansion.

She bought him a driving range coupon, but he wouldn't budge. She gave him the article about the *Titanic* exhibit, but he showed no interest. She wondered what had become of the vibrant young history professor she had married 33 years ago.

"Let's go for a walk," Myrtle would suggest.

"I'm fine here, thanks," was always his reply.

"Frank, if I don't get a chance to have an adventure soon, I just might end up in the nut house with our neighbour, Sandy Crewson."

Myrtle felt dismissed. She had fantasized that retirement would be filled with adventures. Released from the demands of their careers and the responsibilities of parenting, they were equipped with pensions sufficient for world travel. Instead, Myrtle felt herself fossilizing. Each morning her back complained and her knees moved like rusty hinges. Sure, her extra weight didn't help. When she glimpsed her own reflection in a store window she was aghast at the waddling old woman she'd become.

After decades of wearing nurse's scrubs, Myrtle had treated herself to a retirement wardrobe. Her closet contained new tunic tops with bright colours and bedazzled designs. She paired them with elastic-waist pants for maximum comfort, all black to minimize her pear-shaped torso. The dangling sales tags taunted her.

One Sunday evening, as they watched an English vicar solve the weekly murder in his quaint village, an advertisement for Viking River Cruises caught Myrtle's attention. The announcer spoke in a melodic tenor, over a soundtrack of generic waltz melodies, describing the luxury of the floating hotel. Fit, joyful, grey-haired passengers leaned against the ship's railing and gestured toward castles on the passing shoreline. Mature couples laughed together as they enjoyed gourmet meals at tables dressed in crisp white linen. Their frivolity continued as they wandered along cobblestone lanes, interacting with congenial local artisans and shopkeepers. As the day concluded, these geriatric explorers watched fireworks from the ship's rear deck and toasted each other with champagne in elegant glass flutes while gazing lovingly into each other's eyes. Myrtle understood this to be the perfect adventure for her and Frank.

"I think we should go on one of those Viking River Cruises," said Myrtle, standing on her tiptoes, a childhood superstition to ward off unwanted events. "We'd be able to see all sorts of historic sites, like castles and forts, and even ancient battlefields," she added, without concern as to whether this was true.

"I'm fine here, thanks," was Frank's reply.

"But you *love* history. Imagine being able to stand on such ancient ground."

"The ground is the same age everywhere."

"It would be nice to experience some different places." Myrtle sulked. "We never go anywhere."

"We went to your sister's just last weekend."

"That's not the same thing. I need an adventure. I want to experience another world."

"We can do that from the comfort of our own home," said Frank. "There's a documentary on Iceland at 8:00 tonight, and on Friday a six-part mini-series on World War II begins."

The next day Myrtle printed out specifics from the Viking River Cruise website and handed the package to Frank during dinner. With an indulgent sigh Frank scanned the information. The company's vessels were referred to as Viking longships, a clever play on the corporate name and the sleek design scaled for river travel. He noted the ships had state-of-the-art technology, including wireless service and flat-screen televisions with on-demand movie service.

"Hmmmm. According to this I wouldn't need to miss any of my shows," mused Frank. "Maybe it's worth considering."

"Look at the pictures of the staterooms," urged Myrtle, holding a colour image in front of his face. "There are sliding glass doors to private balconies with clear railings so the view is unobstructed. In addition to the bedroom there's a sitting area and a walk-in closet."

"Why would you need a walk-in closet?" asked Frank. "The whole trip only lasts a week. How many clothes are people expected to take?"

"Never mind," responded Myrtle. "Look, there's a spa tub and free bath products, like shower gel and shampoo."

"Nothing's free," grumbled Frank. "It's all built into the price. What does it cost?"

"And look at this." Myrtle poked the page. "There's a sundeck and an observation lounge. They even have a library and boutique shops right on the boat."

"I can bring my own book. What does it cost?"

"They have a laundry service and each night your bed gets turned down and they put chocolate on your pillow. Isn't that elegant?"

"With a walk-in closet full of clothes laundry seems unnecessary. I can turn down my own sheets and buy a chocolate bar if I want one. What does it cost?"

"The boat is so big there are elevators to take you to the different decks. And it says here... there's a hybrid engine for a smoother ride. Imagine, just gliding along the river without a sound." Myrtle sighed as she clasped the printout to her chest.

"What does it cost?"

"The Romantic Danube cruise takes eight days and you see three different countries." Myrtle stabbed a finger at the printout Frank was holding. "The trip begins in Budapest and goes all the way to Nuremberg. It says here we'd see historic architecture, including the Vienna Imperial Palace and Baroque abbeys. The Danube winds through Austria's gorgeous river valleys where we would experience the gracious culture of the area. Doesn't it sound perfect?" Myrtle looked at the photo and held her breath, standing on tiptoe to await Frank's response.

"What... does... it... cost?"

"$2,199.00. That's U.S. dollars... each."

"I'm fine here, thanks," said Frank as he returned to his dinner, now cold and tasteless.

* * *

Myrtle wept for a week. Not straight-out bawling, just little sniffles and sobs. She'd tap a hanky to the edge of her eye, heave a sigh and have a catch in her throat when speaking. She never said her heart had been broken, that disappointment crushed her like a fallen anvil, she felt too proud. She got satisfaction from her martyrdom. For years she had put the needs of others ahead of her own, but she decided that someday, when Frank really wanted something, she'd remind him of his refusal. The following Sunday, while watching public television, the same Viking River Cruise advertisement played, causing Myrtle to flee and lock herself in the master bedroom.

Frank knocked, requesting that Myrtle reappear. For an hour he attempted to coax and cajole her, but she refused access. At last, knowing it was the only solution, Frank agreed to go on a cruise. His only condition was that *he* would do the booking, to see if he could get a bargain. Myrtle instantly agreed.

* * *

As Myrtle suspected, the process of planning the trip captured Frank's imagination. He got swept up in the history related to their itinerary. When the flight landed at the Bergen Airport, they both vibrated with excitement. Frank had explained that their boat would depart from this modest Norwegian port. He'd shown her photos of magnificent fjords and assured her it would be an excellent adventure.

Their taxi passed a busy harbour featuring brightly coloured shops along a cobblestone street. Frank relished the role of tour guide, explaining, "The city was established in 1070, during the reign of King Olav Kyrre. It started as part of his royal estate and became Norway's most important settlement in the 13th century. However, an English merchant ship inadvertently brought the black death here in 1349." Myrtle recalled that her husband had always been a fan of plagues and said a little prayer that nothing would plague this vacation.

Frank spotted the tour sign and led Myrtle in that direction. "Viking Adventures?" asked Myrtle. "I thought the company was Viking River Cruises." She paused, causing pedestrians to disperse around her. "Are you sure this is correct?"

"Viking Adventures. That's right," confirmed Frank. "This company does the same type of trip for *much* less money. It's going to be great." As he held a suitcase in each hand Frank gave Myrtle a nudge with his elbow to get her moving again. "Look! It's a real Viking longship." He prodded Myrtle again and hustled her forward. Her petite round frame bounced through the crowd like a pinball.

When they reached the base of the boarding ramp, Myrtle gawked at the huge ship. It did indeed look like a classic Viking warship, not the floating luxury hotel she had expected. The dark, weathered wood formed the graceful lines of a sea creature. At one end a carved dragon's head with bared teeth looked out to sea. At the opposite end a tail formed a malevolent arch. A row of colourful shields adorned the ship's sides and a canvas tarp sheltered the boat's interior. The sails were bundled to the yardarms and a weathered ramp with rope rails provided access from the shore.

They seemed to be at the right location. Perhaps like a trendy theme hotel, the boat's rustic exterior camouflaged five-star accommodations within. Myrtle looked around, read the multilingual sign at the base of the ramp and evaluated the people around her. Those pushing past her up the gangway were speaking a Nordic language. They seemed young and fit, perhaps part of the crew, she thought. Lifting both of their suitcases Myrtle waddled up the ramp, which Frank had ascended empty-handed.

By the time she climbed to the top Myrtle was wheezing and sweating. She wondered why a luxury enterprise would not have a bellhop. A niggling voice in the back of her mind suggested that something seemed amiss, but she dismissed its poke when she saw how delighted Frank appeared to be.

"Look at this, Myrt!" he nearly shouted. "It's an authentic Viking longboat."

A female crew member greeted guests. With a "Hallo" she handed each visitor a horned helmet, which they immediately donned.

"It's like getting a lei when you arrive in Hawaii," Frank explained.

Guests were also being asked to sign a document. When they reached the front of the line Frank was nearly mesmerized with excitement as he adjusted his helmet. Myrtle carefully put hers in place and began to read the document.

"It's a liability release form," she told Frank. "It says we are agreeing to be a member of the crew and..."

"How fabulous is that!" Frank interrupted. "It's like role-playing. You wanted an adventure, Myrt. Well, this is it! Come on. Let's sign and put these suitcases away." He took a crude writing tool from the ship's greeter.

"Shouldn't we *read* this first?" asked Myrtle.

"No need. It's just standard stuff in case someone gets drunk and falls overboard," said Frank. "No problem for us. Come on. There's a line-up behind us."

* * *

Frank was having the time of his life; Myrtle was doing her best to get with the program. In their tiny cabin they found crew costumes. Loose-fitting layers with heavy leather belts to ensure that one size fit all. When they'd worn the same clothes for two days, Myrtle expressed her concern. Frank reminded her that their clean undergarments minimized any stench.

The dining amenities were not the linen-covered tables, fine china and gourmet meals that Myrtle had hoped for. Frank seemed thrilled. The passengers gathered on benches at long, battered wooden trestles. Roasted root vegetables, parsnips, leeks, carrots and a few unidentifiable items arrived on platters. The first night they were served dark meat, covered in greasy gravy, perhaps goat, certainly not a cow. The second meal had the same vegetables, with boiled fish, white, without embellishment. Warm bread was served with every meal; crusty communal loaves, torn apart by the diners and consumed without butter.

During the day Frank laboured on deck. Myrtle wasn't sure exactly what his tasks involved, but he had been getting fresh air and exercise so she didn't ask questions. Frank and Myrtle were older than most of the crew members, but he kept pace to the best of his ability. They were the only non-Nordic crew, so communication had to be mostly nonverbal. Myrtle didn't see much of Frank during the day because she was required to work in the galley. She peeled and chopped vegetables, washed dishes and helped serve the platters at mealtimes. At first she objected to this labour, but Frank insisted that the participatory nature of the trip kept the cost down, and provided a significant part of the enjoyment. He encouraged her to make note of the recipes.

On the third day at sea, with no shoreline in sight, there a ruckus occurred on deck that drew everyone's attention. Myrtle emerged from the galley with the other women in time to see an elderly man being tied to the mast. Frank sidled over beside her and explained.

"He complained and refused to continue scrubbing the deck," Frank said.

"Did he ask to be transferred to another duty?" asked Myrtle.

"Don't know. They were talking Norwegian, but the guy who supervises us, that big fellow over there with the red beard, looked really annoyed. He yelled and started gesturing like he intended to throw the man overboard."

"Oh my goodness. How awful."

"It's all an act, Myrt. A sort of impromptu skit. I think they've planted actors among us guests," said Frank.

At that moment Red Beard began striking the bound man with a cluster of short ropes. The man wailed in response. After a few lashes he was untied and escorted below deck. Frank thought the performance was spectacular and applauded. Myrtle wondered why the man did not appear at dinner that night.

A restless mood filled the dining hall. People talked in hushed voices. Although Myrtle couldn't understand the language, she recognized the tone of discontent. For the first time flagons of beer were served after dinner. They were refilled upon request and the men became animated. Myrtle noticed some men grab the backside of one of her fellow servers, a young woman with blonde braids and an ample bosom. The amorous advances escalated as adjacent passengers joined in. Myrtle retreated to an alcove, aghast that the serving wench had now been laid across the table. Men waving flagons surrounded the poor woman, tearing at her bodice and lifting her skirts.

"Oh my goodness," whispered Myrtle as she scanned the room to locate Frank. When she looked back to the server being assaulted, Myrtle was shocked to see Frank standing on the table, pouring his glass of beer on the squirming woman while grinning and waving in Myrtle's direction.

* * *

"What on earth were you doing at dinner tonight?" Myrtle used a washcloth to clean her armpits. She'd come to terms with the absence of the en suite spa. "Frank, did you hear me? You men were out of control. Did you hurt that poor woman?"

"It's all part of the role-playing, Myrt."

"Was she an actress?"

"Of course she was. Do you think they'd treat a passenger like that? It's just make-believe. We were pretending to be barbarians. It was fun."

"She didn't look like *she* was having fun."

"She wasn't supposed to. That would have spoiled the effect." Frank rolled over and fell asleep immediately.

"Are you going to sleep in your costume? It's starting to get pretty smelly. And you haven't shaved since we've come onboard. You're starting to look very scruffy. If you keep this up people will think you really *are* a barbarian. I've got to tell you, Frank, this is not the vacation I hoped for. Besides the tiny quarters and crude dining, we haven't even seen a shoreline. No historic walking tours, no quaint shops. I... I want to go home. Frank? Frank, are you awake?"

Her husband's snoring was the only response.

* * *

The next morning a hung-over Frank accompanied Myrtle on her mission to speak with the captain. It was difficult to communicate her wishes to the staff, but when they refused to report to their assigned duties, that got the crew's attention. They were taken to see a large man with a dark beard and a scar over his left eye. He did a lot of yelling, waved his arms and shouted commands.

Myrtle called upon her most diplomatic tone, saying, "We are sorry, Captain, but we seem to have misunderstood the level of... ah... role-playing required on this trip. We are not as young as we once were, and the labour, and lack of mattresses is triggering our health issues. Would it be possible to set us ashore so we can return to our home?"

The captain grunted an angry response.

"Let me try, Honey." Frank stepped forward, offering a slight bow in homage. "I have enjoyed your program very much, but my wife, Myrtle here, is not happy. You know the saying, 'If mama ain't happy, nobody's happy.' So, if it wouldn't be too inconvenient, could we please disembark at the nearest port?"

The captain was silent, which felt even more frightening than his tantrum. He made a single gesture, then Frank and Myrtle were ushered from the room. As they crossed the upper deck Frank noticed the sails were being lowered.

"Do you think he understood us, Frank? These men don't look too happy. We won't ask for a refund. No need to upset them further. I just want to get home, have a bath, and sleep in my own bed... wait a second, where are they taking us?"

"Don't ask questions, Myrt. Keep walking."

"But I don't want to go into the boat's basement."

The man with the red beard gave Myrtle a little shove and she headed down something that was not quite a ladder, yet not fully a set of stairs. She felt shocked to see sweaty, dirty people positioned on benches at oversized oars. It smelled like a mixture of rotting seaweed and decaying meat. Silently, Frank and Myrtle gave each other a sideways glance, then settled into vacant spots. The elderly man to Myrtle's left did not make eye contact and the hunched woman in front of her was groaning.

A large, nearly naked man at the front of the rows stood with his arms crossed, glistening with sweat. He grunted and began slowly beating on a drum, prompting the room's occupants to grab the oars. Frank and Myrtle strained and sweated to the drum's rhythm, then Frank leaned forward and whispered, "Don't worry, Myrt. It's all part of the act." She made a mental note to cancel their cable TV service when they got home.

Caribbean Getaway

I've led a small life. I'd never been on a plane before. The only other country I've travelled to is the United States, and those were road trips. When I was twelve my dad took the family to Florida. We couldn't afford Disneyland, but we did visit an alligator farm. On our honeymoon, Randall, and I drove to Memphis to see the Music Hall of Fame. I never liked country music, but back then I'd have done anything he wanted.

The flight attendant looked like she'd stepped out of a James Bond film. A little hat perched on top of backcombed hair as she minced down the aisle in her tight skirt and high heels, pushing the refreshments cart. She looked like a perfect 1960's stereotype. I felt thrilled to be on this adventure with my best friends.

It had been Celeste's idea for us to go on a girls' getaway. I've known Celeste for 37 years. That's over half of my life. I met her, and Sandy, at university. Their friendship impacted my life path.

Sandy was my roommate. Our friendship evolved until we felt like… twin sisters separated at birth. She had already settled into our dorm room by the time I dragged myself through the door. I was sweaty and exhausted from lugging my worldly possessions up two flights of stairs. I wore a backpack full of books, had a duffle bag over my shoulder and pulled a large wheelie suitcase. Sandy said, "It seems like you have an issue with material possessions." She was unpacking a single suitcase. Her purse and two books sat on the counter that spanned the space between the two single

I dropped my bags and wiped away the ginger hair that had become pasted to my sweaty forehead. I noted my roommate's glossy black hair and perfect complexion. Her bookshelves were full of salty snacks, bottles of wine and a radio with a cassette player. Her collection of tapes included many of my favourites. She had been in the process of pinning a photo of Shaun Cassidy to the bulletin board above her bed. He was the hottest of the Cassidy brothers. The poster showed him wearing a satin jacket with the snaps undone to reveal a bit of his downy chest. His beautiful sandy brown hair was backlit and he seemed to be smiling right at the viewer. Dreamy.

I sat beside Sandy during the flight. Celeste insisted on a seat next to the window, so we put Janice in the middle next to her as punishment. Sandy and I had the aisle and middle seats behind them. The four-hour flight gave us lots of time to reminisce.

To the outside world Sandy and I look nothing alike, but in our hearts we're sisters. We both love the arts. Sandy majored in theatre and I studied visual arts. She dreamed of being a soap opera star, and I wanted to be the next Andy Warhol.

I'd been called Beth my entire life, but Sandy changed that. "What kind of name is Beth?" she asked. "It sounds very Biblical to me. Beth, Faith, Grace, these are not names that will serve you well as a university freshman. Is it short for something?"

"Elizabeth."

"Really? Then why not Liz? Like Elizabeth Taylor. Now,

Marion Reidel appears at top.

Page 184

that's classy. Elegant."

"I'm not really an elegant person," I had said.

"I think you should be Lizzie then," Sandy proclaimed. "Lizzie is jazzy; it's peppy."

I wanted to be sophisticated, but my hometown wasn't the centre of modern culture. Sandy helped me reinvent myself. It only lasted while I attended school; as a mother I slid right back into comfortable old Beth.

Old is how I'd been feeling lately. At 56, I perceived myself as firmly on the downhill side of the slope. Keeping my hair red became a full-time occupation and I've been unable to shed those extra pounds. Buying a swimsuit for this trip was a nightmare, but the remote location of our tropical getaway offered some comfort. I could be sure no one I knew would see my wobbling thighs.

As we listened to Janice chatter in front of us, Sandy and I recalled how we met Celeste. Her roommate, Wendy, had been painfully shy, with all sorts of anxiety disorders, and rarely left their room other than to sit at the back of a lecture hall. So, Celeste teamed up with us. At first I felt a bit jealous. I had a case of *two's company and three's a crowd*, but Celeste always had fabulous ideas for things to do. She's a born social convener. She completed an English literature degree and kept picking up new philosophies to share. It's funny to look back on it now. I remember when Celeste got excited about 'est Training.'

"Werner Erhard is a prophet," Celeste told us. "His theories free people from their past. He wants us to be who we really are, rather than who we think society wants us to be." She ran mini workshops telling us that, "Werner says we are perfect just the way we are, which suits me because changing is way too hard." Celeste only embraced theories that suited her. Years later, I decided not to tell her when Erhard was accused of tax evasion and incest.

I considered Celeste perfect. She was tall and slim, not chubby like me. She loved bright colours and clothes looked fabulous on her. In university she wore her blonde hair long and straight. She had dramatic false eyelashes that made her look like a '60s fashion model. It helped that her parents had tons of money, so she always had something new to wear. Sandy was lucky because she and Celeste were similar enough in size that they could share clothes.

We were the Three Musketeers; confident enough to take on the world. We thought we were in touch with our feelings and the vibrations the universe emanated. It's funny how things turn out.

Celeste and Sandy each married soon after graduation. Celeste said that had been her plan all along. She'd gone to university for her MRS. degree. That's a joke she likes to tell. Celeste loves being the centre of attention. She's good at it. People fall in step behind her without a second thought. She started the Monday Morning Mother's Group. We'd gather with our kids and Celeste's housekeeper would watch them play while we had wine and decompressed. It was like a self-help group. And now, here we are following her again, to an all-inclusive resort.

Before we left home, Sandy and I decided that we'd be roommates at the resort. We sold it to Celeste as a sentimental necessity, but really it served to avoid Janice's intense interaction. Janice means well, but the woman has no off switch and sometimes it's nice just to be silent in each other's presence.

Sandy has become really good at being calm and peaceful. After her marriage breakup she had a little breakdown, but pulled herself together at a meditation retreat. She doesn't like to talk about it. I have a theory that she had a fling with the yoga instructor, but she won't say.

When we arrived, the resort looked spectacular; exactly as advertised. We had adjoining rooms with balconies facing the beach. There was a pool with a swim-up bar and five themed, all-you-can-eat, buffet-style restaurants. Janice always had a plate in her hand. To be honest, we all ate like pigs at a trough.

The beach boys were the best part. They were handsome young locals whose sole purpose was to keep us happy. They would run ahead of us to set up a group of chaise lounges, and they stopped by regularly to adjust the tilt of our umbrella, and make sure we were never without a cool tropical drink. Their beautiful smiles beamed from polished mahogany faces and they spoke with such deference that we felt like royalty.

Celeste repeatedly voiced her desire to take a beach boy home with her. Janice complained that she was the only one with a backyard pool, and wondered why on Earth Celeste would need a beach boy. In response Celeste merely raised an eyebrow. We laughed.

We've joked for years about wanting toy boys. Shit, I guarded my virginity until I turned thirty-one, married Randall out of desperation and had Taylor within a year, only to have him abandon me thirteen years later. Lucky thirteen.

Randall disappeared without a trace and I've been on my own ever since. I joke about wanting a man, but dealing with my kid and rediscovering myself took all my energy.

Sandy has also been single for over a decade. She was forty-five when her husband acknowledged his homosexuality. It devastated her. She's done some online dating, been fixed up by Celeste a couple of times, but no one clicked. Janice and Celeste both retain well-trained spouses. The odds of any of us hooking-up on this holiday were pretty slim, but that didn't stop us from giggling like schoolgirls every time a handsome male approached. We would lie on the beach for hours, weaving fantastic tales of being swept off our feet, yet on the evening when an elegant Latino man offered to buy us drinks, and asked Sandy to dance, we turned into blathering idiots.

On our second-last day we decided to go snorkeling. We'd left the decision a bit late and so the tour group associated with the resort had no vacancies. A taxi driver said that there was a reputable captain in the adjacent village. He would take us for half the cost. We were thrilled.

Celeste had no intention of actually snorkeling—she didn't feel that salt water would be good for her hair—but she wanted to come for the boat ride and said she'd serve as the trip photographer. Janice, Sandy and I were eager to see the coral reef and its colourful inhabitants. We packed our bags with towels and sunscreen, put on our cover-ups, sandals and floppy hats, then squeezed into the taxi. We were ready for an adventure.

The tour office consisted of nothing more than a weathered plank hut with a corrugated metal roof. The exterior was decorated with underwater photos showing outrageously exotic fish and complex coral structures. A faded, hand-painted sign informed us that we'd arrived at Cap'n Randy's Boat Tours. We tipped our driver and discussed pickup plans.

A local woman greeted us, introduced herself as Melia, and took our money. She was a large-bosomed woman in a brightly patterned wraparound dress, with a contrasting patterned cloth encasing her head. Melia led us a short distance to the beach where we could see a grimy fishing boat moored at a rickety dock. Celeste halted. She asked if the vessel had been inspected and certified seaworthy. She wanted to know how many life jackets were onboard and how many years the captain has been conducting tours.

Melia laughed so hard that her entire body jiggled. She said, "Da cap'n es hex-pear-ienced. No worries, lay-dee. You gon ta swim hanyway. Yes?" She continued laughing and jiggling as she walked out on the dock. We followed dragging Celeste.

I could see two men on the boat, neither of them young nor well dressed. They were a shabby pair in bare feet, capri-length pants and faded T-shirts. One man, clearly of African descent, had a greying beard and closely cropped hair. The other was clean-shaven and deeply tanned. The bearded man helped us step aboard and charmed us with his musical island accent. He stowed our bags and drenched us in compliments. He responded to Celeste's inquiries to say that Cap'n Randy has been handling tourists for over a decade. He said, "No worries mahn."

Cap'n Randy came up from below deck. He looked fit and tanned with sparkling eyes and a relaxed smile. He greeted

us with, "Welcome aboard ladies. It's going to be a beautiful…" He froze. The vivid memory of sitting at my kitchen
table with police officers nearly knocked me down. I've pro-
cessed the paperwork to have him declared legally dead, and
yet here he was, my husband Randall. The boat never cast off
that day, but the four of us girls had a spectacular time.

We Drank Wine

Made in the USA
Middletown, DE
22 August 2017